Fall is in the Air

An Oak Harbor Series

Kimberly Thomas

ALL RIGHTS RESERVED. No part of this publication may be reproduced, distributed, or transmitted in any form or by any means, including photocopying, recording, or other electronic or mechanical methods, without the prior written permission of the publisher.

Copyright © 2022 by Kimberly Thomas

This is a work of fiction. Any resemblance of characters to actual persons, living or dead is purely coincidental. Kimberly Thomas holds exclusive rights to this work. Unauthorized duplication is prohibited.

Chapter One

23 Years Ago

R*ing!*
"Hello?"
"Daddy...I-I...I messed up, Daddy."
"Sweetie, where are you?"

Kerry looked up at the neon sign that read "Happy Stay Motel and Apartments."

"I'm in Texas," she spoke into the phone, wiping her face with the back of her hand as her tears flowed unhindered. She'd been sitting on the paved walkway that led up to the motel's lobby entrance since her shift ended at the diner an hour ago. After much contemplation, she'd decided to call her father after ruling out trying to convince the motel manager to give her a day or two to come up with the rent.

"Luke, is that Kerry? Where is she?" she heard her mother ask in the background.

There was a short pause before her mother's voice rang through, "You have to go get her."

"Maria, please…" Luke cautioned his wife. "Are you coming home, sweetie?" he asked, this time directing it to Kerry.

"I can't," Kerry whispered, her voice breaking. She tightened her fingers around the cell phone she'd used her last paycheck to get.

"Do you want me to come and get you?" her father asked calmly.

"Ca-can you?" she replied timidly.

"Of course I will," he affirmed. "Kerry?"

"Yes, Daddy?"

"I love you."

"I…I love you too, Daddy," she choked out past the lump that formed in her throat.

"I'll see you soon."

"Okay, Daddy."

Kerry slowly brought the phone down from her ear as tears blurred her vision. She couldn't believe this was how her life turned out. She hadn't been the straight A, goody-two-shoes child growing up, but nothing she did ever compared to what she'd gotten herself into now. Here she was, sitting outside the complex she'd called home for the past six months, not by choice but because of her boyfriend. After three months of being on the road with him, she'd left everything behind only to be dumped like yesterday's news.

Her eyes became a dam as her mind traveled back to the day he broke her heart.

"Kare Bear, this isn't working out."

"What do you mean?"

"This, us…it's just not working anymore," her boyfriend expressed, pointing from her to him. *"The relationship has run its course."*

"That's not funny, Mark. Why...why are you saying that?"

Her boyfriend stared back at her, unsmiling, his eyes void of the admiration they usually directed at her.

"Why are you doing this?" she asked. The silence was deafening.

Her legs moved her until she was standing before him. Kerry looked deeply into his eyes.

"Why are you doing this?" she repeated. Her hands came up to beat against his leather-clad chest. "Why...why are you... doing...this." She gritted her teeth as she pounded on him.

After a few blows from her hands, Mark sighed, then held her wrists. "It's not you, Kerry."

"Don't you dare say it's a me thing," she threatened.

Mark released her wrists and walked to the rear of the caravan he and his band had been traveling in. "Kerry, you're a nice girl and what we had was special, but this life is not for you. Later down the road, you're gonna realize I did you a favor by letting you go."

"Did I ask you to do me a favor?" she screamed, tears falling down her heated face. "Do you have any idea how much I gave up for you, Mark, huh? In my final year of high school, I had parents who loved me and would do anything for me, siblings, and I gave that all up for you...an-and now...you're dumping me for my own good?" Kerry paced the small kitchenette frantically, trying to make sense of it all. "Why didn't you think about how this would affect me before I threw away my life for you?"

"And there we have it." Mark smirked, clapping his hands mockingly. "I didn't have to wait for a few more months or even a year for you to say that, but it's definitely what's in the back of your mind," he said accusingly. When she didn't say anything but looked back at him as her chest rose and fell rapidly, he continued. "Poor Kerry threw her life away to support her boyfriend in following his dreams. Just admit that this wasn't the life you planned for."

"Of course, this wasn't the life I planned for," she seethed, hugging her chest tightly. "But my dreams changed because I loved you. I thought you would have loved me enough not to break up with me after I dropped everything to be with you for the past three months."

Mark sighed. "Look, I'm sorry that it had to end like this, but better now than later down the road when you've got too much invested in this, and it's even harder to walk away," he reasoned. "I'll give you money to go back to Oak Harbor. You have great parents. I'm sure they'll be thrilled that you came home."

Kerry looked at Mark as if he'd grown another head. "Keep your money," she spat, moving around the small space, taking up the few items she'd brought with her, and stuffing them into her duffle bag. "I made the decision to come here. I'll find my way home without your help."

"Oh, come on, Kerry. Just take the money and go home. Don't make this harder than it has to be," he implored her.

"I'm not making anything harder. I'm simply taking my things and leaving," she spoke airily, moving toward the exit.

"Kerry, don't do this," he tried to reason, walking behind her, but she ignored him. She opened the door to see his bandmates stationed by it, trying to maintain a poker face. "Excuse me," she said simply, then rushed by them. She walked out to the road, and luck would have it that a taxi was coming right at that time.

"Where you headed," the female driver asked her after stopping from her signaling.

"To town," Kerry replied vaguely.

"All right, hop in," the woman welcomed.

Kerry thanked the woman and stepped up into the taxi while ignoring Mark, who was pleading with her to let him help her get home.

"Trouble in paradise?" the woman asked, looking back at Mark as she pulled away.

"What paradise?"

That was the last day she'd seen him. A few weeks later, she received the shock of her life.

Kerry slowly stood and ambled in the direction of the room she currently occupied. She prayed that John, the manager, was too busy to catch her sneaking in. She breathed a sigh of relief when she put the key in the lock, which turned effortlessly. She slipped into the room and turned on the light, releasing another relieved breath. Going to the bathroom, she removed her waitress uniform and stepped into the shower.

Kerry allowed the warm water to run over her hair, her shoulders, and the rest of her body. She lifted her face to the warm water and breathed deeply as it washed away the saltiness from her cheeks. This was the first in a long time she'd felt any kind of hope that everything would be okay. She allowed herself to stay in the shower a little longer, in the warm cocoon of the steam. Her father was coming tomorrow.

The next day

Kerry hugged her hands across her stomach, bringing the baggy sweater she wore in closer contact with her skin. She'd been at the airport for over an hour waiting for her father's arrival.

"Dad," she breathed out the minute she saw him emerge from the terminal gate.

Luke spotted his daughter, and his footsteps faltered as he stared back at her, his eyes bright and cautious as if he expected her to disappear at any minute.

"Hi, baby girl," he spoke softly when he finally stood before her.

"Hi, Daddy," she replied, tears welling up in her eyes. She hadn't realized how much she truly missed her family but having her father standing before her made her both happy and homesick.

Luke reached out with both hands, and Kerry flew into his arms as a flood of tears erupted, unbridled.

"I missed you, Daddy," she said into his chest, her words coming out stifled.

"I missed you too." Her father sighed sadly. "Let's go pick up your things so we can leave," he suggested after they parted.

Kerry widened her eyes before they shuttered, and she stared down at her entwined fingers. "I ca-I can't," she replied.

Luke squinted as his brows furrowed in confusion. "Why not?"

"Because..." She folded her arms over her stomach. She was at a loss for words to explain it, but the sudden sharp intake of breath told her she didn't need to say the words. Kerry braved to look up at her father, whose eyes were directed at a different angle, staring unblinkingly.

"Can we go...to my place?" she asked, fidgeting and pulling the sweater down further as if that could help the situation.

Her father followed her wordlessly outside the airport.

"How did you get here?" she heard him ask from behind her when it was evident she didn't have a car.

"I walked," she replied timidly. Her father didn't say anything more but instead moved in front of her and hailed one of the waiting cabs. After ushering her into the back seat, he got in after her. Kerry gave the driver her address, and he pulled away from the curb. For the remainder of the twenty-minute drive, neither of them tried to get in another word which only put Kerry on edge as she anticipated the incoming argument. She'd glimpsed the disappointment in his eyes that were currently eating away at her like a spider inching closer and closer to its intended meal caught in its web. She wished the earth would just open and eat her whole.

When they made it to the apartment, her father paid the driver and retrieved his luggage. Kerry's heart plunged to the bottom of her chest when she saw John standing at her door, arms folded over each other as he waited for her.

"Ms. Hamilton, this is your last warning. Either you pay

the money you owe by the end of today, or you're out," the man spoke sternly the minute she was in earshot.

"I know, John. I'm sorry. I'm working on it," she promised.

"How much does she owe?" she heard her father ask.

"Four-hundred and fifty dollars," John answered.

She turned to see her father counting out the bills before handing them to the manager.

"This should cover it."

The man nodded in appreciation and walked off in the other direction.

Kerry turned and opened the door, allowing her father to enter. She kept her eyes averted, waiting. She could feel her father's gaze on her but couldn't bring herself to look.

"How far along are you?" he asked, breaking the silence.

Automatically her hand went to touch her stomach. "Um...seven...seven and a half months," she replied, keeping her head down.

"And the father?"

"We broke up six months ago."

"Does he know?"

Kerry shook her head no.

Her father released a long, exaggerated breath before he started pacing back and forth across the carpeted floor. When she didn't hear him moving anymore, she risked a glance only to be caught by his blue eyes looking back at her, disappointment written on his face. The weight of the stare caused her to hang her head in shame.

"You need to call him and let him know that he'll be a father soon," he spoke in a leveled voice.

"I can't," Kerry replied, her voice quivering.

"Kerry-Ann Elizabeth Hamilton, I raised you better than this. You got yourself in this mess, but it wasn't created by yourself only, and now an innocent child is about to come into the world. Call the father," her father commanded in a no-nonsense voice.

Kerry went for the cell phone on the dresser charging and dialed the number that she still knew so well. Her ex-boyfriend picked up on the second ring.

"Hello?"

"Hi, Mark...it's me, Kerry."

"Kerry...wow, I never thought I'd hear from you again," he mused.

"Neither did I," she replied, looking over at her father, who had his arms folded over his chest, watching her.

"To what do I owe the pleasure then?"

"Well, the thing is...um...I'm pregnant, and it's yours."

Chapter Two

Present Day

"Anne, can you please check the oven's timer and tell me how long before the cupcakes are ready?"

"Sure thing, boss."

Kerry stood by the stainless-steel prep table, creaming the butter and sugar in a deep bowl. Satisfied with the consistency of the batter, she reached for the small dish that contained the eggs she needed and began adding them one yolk at a time, folding them into the mixture.

"Fifteen minutes," her employee informed her as she started adding and stirring in the dry ingredients.

"Great. We're right on schedule," she responded, satisfied. She'd been commissioned to bake a birthday cake and cupcakes for a sweet sixteen birthday party that she'd been about to turn down because she hadn't gotten ample notice to prepare it. However, when she saw how distraught the girl and her mother were, her heart gave way, and she decided to do it. Now, here she was at her shop way past her closing hours, baking for a party the next morning.

"You know if you wanna leave, you can go. It's fine," she suggested to the older woman prepping the cake tins at the moment.

"I'm fine," Anne assured her. "Besides, what kind of second would I be if I left you alone in your dire hour of need? Granted, you need to learn to say no sometimes."

Kerry chuckled. "I've got to take a page out of your book Anne."

"That you should do," Anne replied. "Makes no sense you take on more than you can manage. You'll burn yourself right out," she warned. When she was finished with the tins, she walked over to the microwave.

Kerry looked down worriedly at the woman's banded left knee. She'd been diagnosed with arthritis but was adamant she wouldn't let sickness slow her down. "Why don't you sit for a while? I'll get the butter," she offered.

Anne waved dismissively. "It's fine. I'm already there anyhow."

"Okay," Kerry relented, turning her attention to the batter. After a few more mixes, she was satisfied with the consistency. She brought the cake tins closer and began pouring even amounts into each. She looked over to see Anne creaming the butter and sugar to make the frosting to top the cupcakes.

The timer went off, indicating that the cupcakes were done. Kerry slipped her hands into the mittens before opening the industrial oven. The heat from the caverns rushed out to blast her in the face. She removed the trays and placed them on the counter before resetting the timer and slipping in the cake tins.

Her cell phone vibrated in her pocket, and she straightened to retrieve it.

"Hello?"

"Hi, Mom."

"Hi, sweetie," Kerry replied, a smile brightening her face at her daughter's voice. "How are you? How's school? Anything interesting to tell me?"

"Mom, one question at a time." Her daughter laughed. "I swear, every time I call, it's literally twenty-one questions as if we didn't just go over the same topics a few days before." Her daughter continued to chuckle.

"A lot can happen in a few days," Kerry said with a smile, happy to know that despite her many questions, her daughter didn't view it as an invasion of privacy.

"All right, so my answers are, I'm fine, school's great, and no, nothing interesting has happened since we last spoke, and that includes boys."

It was Kerry's turn to chuckle at the last part of her daughter's response. "You know me so well."

"Like the back of my hand," her daughter replied. "I was calling to tell you I'm coming home after midterms. It feels like I've been at school forever even though it's fall, and the term just started."

Kerry grinned appreciatively at her daughter's news. "I'm looking forward to seeing you too, sweetie. You don't know how much I miss you already."

"I know, Mom," her daughter snickered.

"Hey," Kerry responded in an offended tone.

"Love you, Mom."

Kerry smiled again. "And I love you, my star. Just remember not to work yourself to a nervous breakdown. No matter what happens, I'll always support you. Do your best. I'm already proud of you."

"I know, Mom," Sophia replied after a short pause.

Her mind flashed to her tenuous relationship with her parents in the latter years of her teens. Though they were on good terms now, there was a time when they couldn't see eye to eye, and they didn't support her choices which ultimately led to her making some life-altering decisions that still affected her to this day. Since the day each of her daughters was born, she'd decided that she wouldn't make the same mistake she believed her father had made with her.

"I love you, sweetie," she spoke with much feeling.

"I know, Mom. I love you too."

After a few seconds of emotional silence, Kerry asked, "Have you heard from your sister?"

"Um yeah, she video called me two days ago to show me that she was at 'Les Catacombes des Paris.'"

Kerry laughed at her daughter's pronunciation of the word. "So, she's in France then."

"Yup," Sophia replied, popping the *P*

"Well, here's to hoping she'll remember she has a mother. Maybe she'll call me soon," Kerry replied, her tone dry.

"You know that's how she is, Mom. She'll call you."

"I suppose you're right." She wanted to give her children the freedom to make their own choices and mistakes. She wanted them to chart their own courses, unlike how it had been for her for a good period of her adult life. But occasionally, she wondered if she had given Emma a little too much freedom to do so. She guessed time would tell.

"Mom, I gotta go. I'll talk to you soon."

"Okay, sweetie. Be safe."

"Always."

The two ended the call, and Kerry returned to finishing her baking. She and Anne didn't leave the shop until after ten that night. When she got home, she quickly rinsed off and donned her pajamas. She fell into her bed, bone tired.

The following morning, Kerry went for a run before heading to her bakery. Leaving her apartment complex on Crosby Avenue, she headed for N. Oak Harbor Street, then turned onto NE 10th Ave., keeping a steady pace. She relished these early morning runs. She was out before the sun was ready to peep out from its hiding place behind the mountains and back home before it shone in all its glory overhead.

Kerry's feet made contact with the concrete pavement pushing her forward. She breathed in deeply, filling her lungs with much-needed oxygen and releasing the toxic air that had built up periodically. She loved the cool air dancing across her face. It felt exhilarating as she powered down the straight. As predawn gave rise to the first rays of sunshine, she turned in the direction of home. The Cascade Mountain Range stood before her, separated in the distance by a wall of tall evergreens, Great Oaks, and water so transparent it made the mountain itself seem as if it was rising out from it. It brought attention to its magnificent, ridged rock face scattered with trees and low shrubs. She took in the ice-capped tips that blended in with the fluffy clouds that clung to its peaks. Oak Harbor had some glorious sights to tantalize the senses. It was truly a wonderful place to live. As much as she'd been the adventurous type and was trying to return to that side, she loved the pace of the little coastal town.

After her run, Kerry took a shower and donned a blue, floral-printed dress that stopped at her knees and flared. She brushed her platinum blond pixie cut back so that the strands fell behind the curves of her ears, the length not putting it further than just above the lobes. She inserted two gold knobs in each ear and selected a pair of flat, silver, strapped sandals before heading for the door. After removing her key from the hanger by the door, she exited her unit and took the one flight of stairs down to the lobby.

"Good morning, Ms. Hamilton."

"Good morning, Jefferey. How are you?" she greeted the concierge, who had a welcoming, radiant smile plastered on his lips.

"I'm fine, Ms. Hamilton." Kerry gave him a smile of understanding before heading for the exit. When she made it to her red-and-white Mini Cooper, she entered the vehicle and drove down Main Street, heading onto the I-20. Five minutes later, she was at the intersection of Midway Blvd and Goldie Road, and two seconds later, she was pulling up to her bakery. Above the red-and-white awning that arched over the front of the single-story, red brick building was the sign in bold confetti colors, "Heavenly Treats"— her baby. She took a few minutes admiring what seventeen years of marriage and a divorce settlement had gotten her. Most of the outer brick wall was covered by Boston ivy and honeysuckle blossoms. Wide, paneled, glass windows gave a limited view of all the treats on the inside, already out in full display. If that wasn't enough, the scent of cinnamon, nutmeg, and the other spices that were key ingredients in most baked goods floated in the air. They tickled her nostrils with their tantalizing aroma— an indication that Anne was already there baking. It may not have looked like much to others, but to her, it was everything.

She walked down the path marked by her potted plants to push the glass door open and step into the bakery. She rounded the counter and pushed open the iron door that led to the kitchen. Anne stood by the counter, kneading dough.

"Why is it that no matter how hard I try, you're always here before me?" Kerry asked the woman as she reached for the apron from the top drawer of the small chest in the corner, furthest away from the heat.

"That's because I'm psychic," Anne replied, shrugging. She didn't bother to look up from what she was doing, but Kerry could see the corners of her mouth tilted in a smile or a smirk. She wasn't sure.

"Mark my words, Anne. I will beat you to it one day," she promised.

"You can try," the older woman replied, the challenge evident in her tone. "I would love to see the day that you actually get here before me.

Fall is in the Air

Kerry rolled her eyes playfully. "Don't get overly confident now, Anne. You might just live to eat your words," she parlayed. She washed her hands and went to the refrigerator to remove the icing and fruit she would add to the cake for the birthday party. She'd already layered it, so the only thing left was to decorate it.

The chiming of the bell at the front caught her attention. "I'll go," she informed Anne, who was straightening up to do the same. The woman nodded and returned to flattening the dough to cut it into rollable portions.

"Welcome to Heavenly Tr— Faith? What's wrong?" she asked the petite woman who owned the toy store two shops away from hers, standing by the counter looking perturbed.

"This," the woman replied, waving what looked like a flyer. Kerry took it from her and read the content, her eyes widening as she realized what it was saying.

"Where did you get this?" she asked the woman, alarm sounding in her voice.

"It's posted on every notice board around town."

"These people won't quit," she responded, her annoyance evident. She looked back at the flyer inviting the small business owners to a town hall meeting by the investors of Major Corp to sensitize the populace on their aim to acquire their businesses, tear them down and build something foreign to the area. She would go to the town hall meeting all right, but it was to tear into them for trying to force the sale down their throats.

Chapter Three

"All you big shot companies are doing is coming into town and destroying it with your conglomerates. Pretty soon, the town will lose its authenticity, and I'm not for it."

There were shouts of approval from the other business owners and residents that turned out for the town hall meeting at the Oak Harbor Conference Center downtown. The man who'd spoken held up his fist as an act of defiance before taking his seat.

One of the men sitting on the podium rose to his feet and brushed down his suit before standing in front of the mic. "Residents of Oak Harbor, we at Major Corp believe fully in community development. It is not our intention to work against you but rather with you." The man held up his hand, requesting that the people that had started to murmur let him finish.

Kerry sat at the back with her arms folded over her chest as she listened carefully to what the suits had to present.

"We do intend to build a shopping mall and conjoining

parking lot but...but we do plan on incorporating green spaces in our design to better cater for families."

Kerry rolled her eyes. She knew what that meant— usually, a mini-golf park or flower garden that did nothing to the interest of the people.

"Let's face it, the town is dying. Young people are leaving in droves to find better opportunities elsewhere, the town's GDP is below most towns that are its size— pretty soon, other companies will come in and want to build where your shops are, and they won't be so caring about your interests."

Again, Kerry rolled her eyes, her annoyance almost at peak level. The murmurs of the people began to drown out what the man was saying.

"If you allow us to buy your shops at a price that will benefit you, at least what we're building will bring back jobs into the community and help alleviate brain drain."

Again, there was a great uproar from the residents. Kerry decided that she'd heard enough, stood, and waited for the noise to die down.

"Yes, you in the back," the moderator pointed her out.

"What assurance do we have that you aren't shortchanging us?" she asked with her hands folded. "As far as we know, the plans that you're pedaling to us are bound to change the minute the ink dries on the pieces of paper you give to us, and we, as the residents of Oak Harbor, are left with nothing."

"Ma'am, we understand your concern, but as I said before, we wo—"

"You don't have to say anything else. I will not be selling my business, and there is no way I am allowing you to take it. We, the citizens of Oak Harbor, are no fools, and we will not allow you to take away what we've worked hard to maintain all these years."

There were cheers of approval as she turned and made her way toward the exit.

"Ladies and gentlemen, please, if you would take your seats and let us finish this meeting amicably."

Kerry looked behind her to see most of the other people had risen from their seats and were walking toward the exit as well, staging a walkout. A small triumphant smile lifted her lips. That would teach them to think that they could be bought.

Realizing that she had some time on her hands, Kerry decided to visit her parents. Her dad had indicated that they would be home for the day. It was as good a time as any as her mother had been begging her to visit for months. Stopping by the bakery she'd closed to attend the meeting, she removed the cheesecake from the refrigerator and boxed it up to take with her. Ten minutes later, she was on N. Torpedo Road, and two minutes later, she made a left turn unto W. Crescent Harbor Road, traveling eastbound. In less than three minutes, she pulled into the graveled driveway of her parents' two-story colonial-style home. In all her years, the house had never deviated in appearance. The sprawling home still maintained the same robin's egg blue color with sandpaper-colored gable roofs with the edges trimmed white. The French windows were also trimmed white; however, the front door painted bright purple was ostentatious enough to break up the house's uniformity.

Happy memories invaded her thoughts of the family sitting close to the fireplace in the family room, singing Christmas carols and telling funny stories. Her parents would stick marshmallows on maple skewers for them to roast over the flames in the hearth. Everyone was decked out in the ugly sweaters that Aunt Stacey made each year for her and the extended family. Her smile broadened as she remembered how her brother Charles would get her to give him her marshmallows by tricking her that she needed to leave some for Santa, or he wouldn't leave any presents for her for being mean. Little had her five-year-old self known that her brother was conning her because his booty had finished, but as she grew older, she caught on to his tricks. She laughed as she exited the car and took the three stone steps that led up to the porch. She purposely walked to the door and knocked. A few moments later, the door swung open.

"Oh, honey. You came." Her mother beamed up at her.

"Hi, Mom," she greeted, slightly bending to give her a kiss on her cheek, holding the cake box away from their slight embrace. "I promised I would visit."

"I know, dear, but it's been months," her mother pointed out as she ushered her inside. "Getting to see you a little bit more wouldn't be so bad. Your sister and brothers visit regularly, and they've got pretty busy schedules."

"Well, they're them, and I am me." Kerry shook off her jacket and placed it in the small coat closet off to the side, just behind the front door. "We all can't be the perfect mom."

"That's not what...I didn't mean to imply..."

"It's fine," Kerry assured her. She heard her mother sigh. Knowing that she was going to try to apologize again and make the already awkward situation even more awkward, she whirled to face the woman with a bright smile. "I brought cake," she revealed, holding the box in her two hands before her.

"Thank you," her mother replied, with a small grin, reaching to take the box from her.

"It's your favorite," Kerry tacked on. "I bet you won't wait until after dinner to have a piece." She smirked knowingly.

"Are you trying to get me fat?" her mother asked with a chuckle.

"Mom, if you were destined to be any heavier than you are right now, I'm sure it would have happened a long time ago. Just eat cake and celebrate your metabolism."

Her mother gave her a warm smile, the tension from earlier forgotten. "Are you staying for dinner?" she asked. "Charles and Sharon are stopping by as well."

Kerry thought about it. "Sure," she confirmed. She knew that if she had refused, it would have led to another transgression added to her ever-growing rap sheet. She followed her mother through the broad archway that opened to the kitchen. She sat on of the bar stools stationed by the island that split the kitchen in two. "Where's Dad?" she asked, looking around as if she expected him to pop through the archway.

"He's out back chopping firewood," her mother informed her as she unboxed the cake. She transferred it to a cover plastic and slipped it into the fridge.

"What for?" Kerry asked, sitting up straight on the stool.

"That's just something he does. He makes sure that the woodshed remains stocked in case of an emergency." Kerry nodded in understanding.

"Why don't you come and help me? I was just about to start making dinner," Maria invited.

"Okay," Kerry agreed, taking the apron she offered. "What do you need me to do?" she asked, coming to stand by the granite counter to await instructions.

"You can start by washing the vegetables, then julienne them," her mother instructed. "I'm making steak, mashed potatoes, and a vegetable casserole."

Kerry did exactly as her mother asked, the two working in sync to put the meal together. "I remember when you were just two, you used to come in the kitchen, sit and watch me cook until you were able to prepare a whole meal without my help, but you always wanted me by your side when you did."

"I remember." Kerry smiled fondly at the memory. "I think that's where I got my love for cooking and then baking— from you."

Her mother smiled knowingly before the corners of her mouth turned down slightly. "But then you hit your teens, and we spent less time together in the kitchen until one day you just stopped altogether."

Fall is in the Air

Her mother's drooping eyelids said more than her words could ever convey, and Kerry felt a pang in her heart. She remembered why she had decided to stop cooking, and now she realized that it was the exact moment her relationship with her mother had started to dwindle.

"Hmm, something delicious in here," Luke called out as he made his entry into the kitchen.

"Hi, sweetie. I didn't know you were here."

"Hey, Dad. I had some time on my hands, so I chose to come and visit you old folks."

"Hey, who are you calling old?" her father asked in mock indignation. "I bet you can't take me in a test of fitness," he challenged, bobbing and weaving as if he was a boxer.

"Bring it on, old man," Kerry countered, putting her hands up in a defensive stance.

Her father playfully tapped her hands, and Kerry lithely jumped back on her feet as laughter erupted from her lips as her father skipped from one foot to the next.

"Not in my kitchen!" Maria called out warningly.

"Looks like I got here just in time."

The two turned to see Charles at the archway with his hands folded across his chest, a broad smile on his face.

"Dad was just saying he's still got it," she filled her brother in, cheekily adding, "even though he's as old as time."

"Hey," their father bellowed, straightening up with a childlike pout.

"I bet he thinks he's Rambo. What do you say, old man? Do you think you can take on the both of us at once?" Charles asked, walking over to stand beside Kerry.

"Bring it on," their father dared.

Charles removed his jacket, loosened his tie, and rolled his shirt sleeves up to his elbows.

"Why do you always get like this?" their mother asked, throwing her hands in the air, shaking her head in disapproval.

Still, the siblings and their father paid no attention to her as they bobbed and weaved and sent out light punches toward their father, who effortlessly blocked it before sending out his own. At the end of the game, they all doubled over on the floor in a fit of laughter and trying to catch their breaths. Kerry was the first to lift herself from the ground and reached down to pull the other two up.

"I concede, Dad, you're right. You've still got it," she said, raising her hands in defeat.

"Yeah, Dad, you're still Ninja warrior number one," Charles jumped in to say, a snicker escaping his lips at the end. This triggered Kerry's laughter, and she held on to her brother's shoulder, her other hand over her tummy as she doubled over with laughter.

She relished moments like these when they could laugh freely and have weightless fun as a family unit as they were now few and far between. Too many words spoken and unspoken had left their relationship teetering on edge more often than not.

"So, did you decide to sell your little business to the corporation?" her father asked after the laughter had died down.

And just like that, the moment passed, and the mood shifted.

Chapter Four

"Kerry's here!"

Kerry shook her head at the grand announcement by her sister Tessa, rolling her eyes playfully at the cheers that erupted. She'd stood by the porch column, looking out at the scene before her and reveling in the fact that despite their differences, her family always showed up to support each other, just like now. Ever since her cousins Cora, Andrea, and Josephine had returned to the island, things had been different. The family get-togethers felt more whole, more meaningful. It was just too bad that it had to take the death of her uncle, Sam, the girl's father, to evoke this change.

"Did you bring the cakes?" her cousin Cora asked while greeting her with a hug.

"Oh no! I knew I forgot something," she replied, holding her cheeks in her hands as her mouth and eyes widened in shock.

"Shoot," Cora responded with disappointment. Her eyes lit up a little while after. "We still have time to go get them, the party's just getting started, and it's literally just a thirty-minute drive to and from the bakery," she suggested.

"Cora, relax. The cakes are here. I was just kidding." Kerry laughed.

Cora gave Kerry's shoulder a gentle shove. "You're not nice," she said with a serious face, but the light spark in her blue-gray eyes gave it away that she wasn't serious.

"Never darling, never," Kerry replied, doing her best Cruella de Vil imitation. "Can you do something for me?" she asked seriously.

Cora raised a curious brow at her. "What about?" she asked.

"Could you do maybe an expose on the small businesses in the business district, how they provide value to the town and how Major Corp acquiring our businesses will lead to total disaster?"

"Say no more," Cora replied, her eyes twinkling, the journalist in her already activated.

"Thanks, Cor." The two walked off to join the others.

Kerry sat in one of the wicker chairs under the pergola. Her niece Dianne brought over a root beer which she instantly opened and took a few sips of.

"How did it go at the town hall?" Dianne asked as she leaned against the wooden post that formed a part of the pergola's foundation.

"They basically repeated the same information that they sent out last year about buying our business, turning it into something that will encourage more traffic to the business district, yada yada yada," Kerry answered, shaking her head.

Dianne hugged her hands over her chest, bobbing her head contemplatively. After more than a minute, she spoke again. "Do you think they have what it takes to force us out of business?" she asked, biting her bottom lip.

"Absolutely not," Kerry refuted with confidence. "I'll fight tooth and nail to ensure that doesn't happen," she assured her.

Dianne nodded in agreement.

"Your bistro was the breakout business this quarter, and it's been doing great, Dianne. I know how much sweat and tears it took for you to get it off the ground. Remember?"

"It's because you talked to Mom and got her to loan me the start-up," her niece spoke in appreciation.

"That was the easy part," she brushed off. "You did the heavy lifting, and you proved your tenacity to your mother."

"Still, I know I couldn't have done it without you."

Kerry grinned at the young woman. She was proud of her for persevering amid all the naysayers and the resistance she got. Java Bistro was what it was because her niece believed in herself and her dream. It hit her then that her family, mainly the parents, usually tried to get them to do and become what they would have envisioned for them since birth. Usually, deviating from the chosen path led to ostracization like what happened to Cora and her sisters and their father, constant reminders of the mistakes that you made, like with her and her father, her sister Tessa, and her brother Brian, not with the career change their children made. She wasn't left off the list, but she was trying her best to be understanding and patient with Emma, who reminded her so much of herself at that age. She only prayed that she would be careful and that she wouldn't be weighed down by regret in the end.

"You could have done it without me, Dianne. You have a fire in you that no one can extinguish," she informed her niece.

"Thanks, Aunt Kerry."

Kerry smiled encouragingly and opened her arms to her. Dianne fell into the embrace.

"You know you're my favorite aunt, right?"

"I'm your only aunt," Kerry laughed.

"That makes me uttering it even more special then," the young woman reasoned.

Kerry cackled.

After Dianne left to go help her fiancé Jared set up the volleyball net, Kerry turned her attention to the activity at the grill.

Her father was stationed there, flipping pieces of meat. The black oak wood crackled in the lower cavity of the grill, sending up a smoky, sweet aroma, infusing the marinated meats as they sizzled over the grill grates. She felt her mouth salivate; she was literally tasting the meat from the aroma penetrating her olfactory receptors. She wanted to go grab a plate and get a piece of the meat. However, she remained seated. Kerry didn't want to interact with her father because she was still hurting from their last conversation two days ago.

She couldn't understand how, after all this time and proving herself to have made the right choice to open her own bakery, her father still viewed it as a hobby that wasn't meant to be a long-term career. She'd been disappointed by his comments. The whole dinner afterward had been filled with tense words and awkward silences. The minute she had finished, she'd bolted, not wanting to say something that she would end up regretting in the end.

"How are you?" She looked up to see her mother staring at her with concern marring her face.

"I'm fine, Mom," she answered simply, looking back down, then taking a few more sips from the can in her hand.

Her mother seemed to take that as an invitation to occupy the empty chair to her right. The two sat in silence for some time before her mother spoke up. "Your father loves you, sweetie, and he has always wanted the best for you. It's just that sometimes he doesn't think before he speaks."

Kerry snorted at the understatement of the year. Her

mother released a soft sigh. "I know that the years that have passed can't make up for what happened, but—"

"Mom, please." She stopped her mother from continuing with what she was about to say. "This has nothing to do with... what happened or my feelings about it. This is about Dad not taking me or my bakery seriously. I worked hard to get it, to make it what it is, and for him to ridicule and minimize my accomplishments really hurts. I'm not a kid anymore. I'm a forty-one-year-old divorced woman who's grown two children to adulthood. I believe I get the right to choose what is best for me." Her voice quivered at the end as she tried to control her emotions.

Maria placed her hand over her daughter's folded ones. Kerry turned to look at her, the pain shining through her emerald eyes. "I'm sorry that your relationship is constantly plagued by this tension. Your father is set in his ways, and that leads to him hurting the people he cares about the most. I know it's hard to get along, but can you try?"

Kerry looked away from her mother for a moment.

"Please, sweetie. Just try," Maria implored.

Kerry sighed. "I'll try," she promised. Her mother gave her arm a light, encouraging squeeze before rising from the chair. "I'm gonna check on Becky," she said, heading for the house. Kerry exhaled as she stared over at the man standing by the grill. She wished that getting along with her father came as easy as breathing.

She decided to table her attempts at civility to her father for later. She turned her head to observe the others.

A smile came to her lips when she realized that her cousins were all paired up and looking happy. Cora sat by the unlit hearth blushing at whatever Jamie was whispering to her, and when she looked down toward the bay, she saw Andrea and Donny walking hand in hand. The sisters had all been struck by love since returning to the island. Now they were in fresh, healthy relationships with men that treated them with love and respect. Compared to what they had before and how it ended, she could see that the relationships they were in now suited them the best.

"I told you it wouldn't work."

Kerry looked over at her cousin Ben who was sprawled on the grass with Marg standing over him with a knowing smirk. She reached her hand out, and Ben begrudgingly took it to allow her to help him up. "Oh, don't be mad. I'm glad you tried to do it for me," the woman cajoled, hugging her cousin tightly. "Want a kiss?" she asked when Ben continued to pout. His lips turned up into a smile as he nodded in response. Marg laughed and placed her lips against his cheek.

A soft smile came to Kerry's lips as she looked at her cousin being in a wholesome relationship. Marg was a lovely woman that she liked very much. She had literally become family, and Kerry couldn't see Ben with anyone more lovely. After all he'd been through in his first marriage, he deserved to be happy.

"Who's in for a game of cards?"

Kerry felt herself unconsciously roll her eyes at her father's question. It was obvious that it would take more than just a pep talk from her mother for her not to be annoyed with the man. She supposed, at the most, she needed to cool off for a few more days.

She rose to her feet and headed for the house. She found Cora's daughter Julia sitting in the old rocking chair on the porch, a faraway look on her face.

"Are you okay, sweetie? Why aren't you with the others?" she asked.

Julia shook her head before looking at her. "I just needed some time to myself," she replied, lips pursed.

Kerry drew closer to her. "Whatever it is, I want you to know that I'm here for you. If not me, you have a whole host of family who will be," she encouraged her.

"Thanks," Julia replied with a small smile that didn't reach her eyes. Kerry smiled back at her.

"How's the baby?" she asked, looking down at the girl's slightly rounded tummy made evident by the midi bodycon dress she wore.

Julia focused her eyes on the bump and released a tired sound. "Kicking up a storm," she replied.

Kerry felt her heart heave with compassion for the young woman. She bent forward and placed a comforting hand on the girl's shoulder. "Everything will work out. You just have to keep your spirit up for you and this baby."

Julia looked up at her; this time, her eyes pooled with tears.

"We're all here for you," she informed Julia, running her palm against her cheek comfortingly.

Chapter Five

Kerry stood by the cash register, lost in her thoughts. Her day hadn't started off the way she wanted. She'd been informed that one of the shop owners was seen having dinner with one of Major Corp's top representatives the day before, and she knew that could only mean one thing; the man was thinking of selling his business to them. If more shop owners started doing the same thing, then they would lose the support that they had in numbers and would definitely have to consider selling.

Kerry reached down to retrieve her vibrating phone, and her eyes furrowed at the caller ID.

"Hello?" she answered.

"Hey, Kerry. How are you?"

She removed the phone from her ear and rechecked the caller id.

"What is it, Darren?" she asked, her voice ringing with annoyance.

"Well, hello to you too," her ex-husband replied, matching her annoyance.

Kerry sighed. "What do you need, Darren?" she responded tiredly.

She could hear shuffling in the background.

"I was wondering if you were free for lunch?" he asked.

Kerry squinted in confusion. "Why? We aren't even friends."

"Kerry, we might not be close anymore, but I do still care about you," he returned.

She narrowed her eyes in suspicion. "What do you want, Darren?"

After a few seconds of silence, her ex-husband exhaled. "I need your help with something," he relented.

Kerry remained silent, waiting and knowing that she had the upper hand. If he had to ask her for something, then that meant he was in deep trouble because she was certain she was the last person he would contact.

"I need someone that I can trust. The books at the office need to be checked before a CPA comes in. Something just isn't adding up. I know when you were in accounting, you always paid attention to detail and could find the tiniest discrepancy. So, what do you say? Will you help?"

Kerry laughed hysterically. "I never thought the day would actually come that Darren Johnson would need my help with anything...I recall that you said the day you ever asked me for anything ever again would be the day that hell froze over. Has hell frozen over?"

There wasn't any answer from the other end of the line for a good ten seconds.

"Look, Kerry. I didn't call to dredge up what I said or to fight. God knows we've done a lot of that in the past few years. I just need to know if you'll help me."

"And what is this help worth to you?" she asked, leaning her back against the counter.

"What do you mean?" he asked in a perplexed voice.

"I'm talking money, Darren," she answered. "You want me to take time out of my busy schedule to help you with a problem that no longer has anything to do with me. We're not married anymore, remember? So, if I am offering my services to you, it is on a work-for-hire basis."

"You're unbelievable," Darren returned bitterly. "After all we've been through. After all I've done for you and the fact that I have to pay alimony, you want me to hire you to do the work that ensures you get those checks every month?"

Kerry sank the base of her palm into her eye and rubbed, feeling a tension headache just on the horizon. That's how it always turned out whenever she talked to Darren.

"Look, Darren. I really don't have the time to go back and forth with you. I'm already having a crappy day, so either you pay for the service or get someone else that will work for free," she shot.

"You know what? I'm sorry I even called you," he flung back at her.

"Makes two of us," she retorted just before he hung up the phone in her ear.

Kerry sighed as she pocketed the phone. So much for civility, she thought to herself. Just as she started to walk off, her phone vibrated against her leg. She fished it out and rolled her eyes when she saw who was calling.

"Yes, Darren?" she said noncommittally.

"What figure are we looking at here?" he asked, his voice businesslike.

"Just pay me half of what you would pay any other accountant," she proposed.

"Okay," Darren agreed. "Does that mean you'll meet me for lunch?"

"Absolutely not," Kerry deadpanned.

She heard his laughter as she removed the phone from her ear and pressed the End Call button. She moved in the direction of the kitchen, deciding to bake and blow off some steam.

Kerry put on her apron and washed her hands before she opened the large, double-door industrial fridge to get the ingredients she needed.

For the next two hours, she whisked, creamed, kneaded, and rolled batter and dough. The bell at the front chimed, indicating that someone was in the shop. Dusting off some of the flour from her apron, she went to serve whoever it was.

"Something smells really good in here."

"It's a bakery, Sylvie. It's meant to smell that way," Kerry said, sarcasm in her voice. "I would be worried if it didn't," she added.

The woman gave her a wry smile. "I just meant that whatever you have around there is making me anxious to feed my sweet craving."

"So, you're here to buy something?" she asked, cocking an eyebrow.

"No," the woman replied. She breathed in deeply before releasing it and setting serious eyes on Kerry. "I think we have a problem."

Kerry furrowed her brows. "What kind of problem?" she asked.

The woman shook her head slightly in disappointment. "Mr. Harriott, the tearoom owner back on third, he signed the sale agreement they gave him, and Mrs. Bell also caved."

"No," a dismayed Kerry responded.

"Yes, and I heard that a few more owners are thinking of selling too."

Kerry couldn't believe that what she feared was taking fruition. "And how do you feel?"

Sylvie reared back as she fixed Kerry with an offended gaze. "I am a true Oaker through and through. More than three generations of seniors have lived and thrived here. This business has always been in my family. There is no way I would ever sell to a conglomerate," the woman who owned the novelty store just to the left of the bakery spoke passionately.

"I'm sorry. I didn't mean to imply that you were considering doing that," Kerry apologized. "It's just been so hard trying to remain positive, especially knowing how these big companies operate. They just add a few more zeroes to their offers, and people begin tripping over themselves to sign away something that should have meant more to them than the money."

"I know it's hard, Kerry, but we've got to keep hopeful and not turn on each other."

Kerry nodded in agreement. She just wished she knew what the others were feeling.

* * *

Kerry stood in the heavily wooded mountainside of Goose Rock Trail and inhaled deeply. She could smell the freshness of the air coupled with the smell of the damp earth and decaying leaves that would dissolve completely into it to add nourishment to the roots of the same trees they had fallen from. She loved the musky, woodsy scent. It calmed her to be enraptured by nature, allowing the problems from life to fade away and giving rise to a more primitive desire to become one with it all as she emersed herself in the sight, sounds, and smells of the forested trail.

She had been meandering her way through the trail for the past hour, but it would soon be time to return home and back to reality. She propelled herself forward, running her hands over the woody barks of the trees. The leaves were a deep green hue that turned down to look at her. She could hear the chirping of birds calling to their mates and rustling here and there of the shrubs where small animals seemed to be hiding.

Fall is in the Air

She made it to the clearing that looked out at the blue-green waters. She lifted her head to the morning sun to allow it to heat up her skin. She wished she had a paraglider right in that instance to free herself, even more, to glide over the water's surface.

After another fifteen minutes of staring out at the ocean, Kerry turned and made her way back down the trail. She got into her car and drove home to prepare to go to the bakery after freshening up. She was glad that she'd decided to go for a hike to clear her mind because today, she felt rejuvenated, ready to take on the problems as they came, and knowing that she had what it took to make it.

After a long, hot shower, she donned a pair of black denim jeans and tucked her white, button-down shirt-blouse into the waist. Staring at her reflection in the mirror, she used her hand to smooth back her blond hair that was in between a pixie cut and a chic bob to bring attention to her diamond-shaped face with her high cheekbones, her deep-set sultry green eyes, and a long, thin nose over her small, heart-shaped lips. Kerry wasn't vain, but she had to admit that she looked really good for her age.

Ten minutes later, Kerry slipped into a pair of black flats, grabbed her keys, and headed for the lobby. Two minutes later, she was pulling out of the apartment complex and headed for the bakery.

"Good morning, Anne. How was your day off?" she asked her second in command the minute she walked into the kitchen.

"Not what I expected," the woman replied, making a face.

Kerry looked over at her as she tied her apron behind her.

"I had to babysit my grandchildren," she gave by way of explanation. "I have never seen a more rambunctious set in my whole life," she continued, shaking her head.

"Admit it, you love having them around." Kerry laughed. "Why else would you take them every week?"

"Because I am a sucker for punishment," the woman whined.

"Yeah, well, you made that bed, so don't complain too much about it."

"I won't...I'm not," Anne replied. "Before I forget, a new order came in today. They need a cake and pastries for a baby shower."

"Okay, when exactly is this?" she asked.

"It's this weekend," Anne informed her, pointing to the reminder stuck on the refrigerator door.

"All right," she replied.

The two women turned to their respective stations to prep for the baking for the day. They had about two hours before the shop would open to customers. After sticking the cinnamon buns into the oven, Kerry removed her apron.

She felt her phone vibrate in her jeans pocket. Fishing it out, her face scrunched up in confusion at the strange foreign number. "Hello?" she answered.

"Hi, Mom."

A smile lit Kerry's face at the sound of her daughter's voice.

"Hi, honey," she responded, turning and resting her back against the cold granite countertop. "How are you?" she inquired.

"I'm great. I just wanted to call you and let you know that I am fine."

"I appreciate that." Kerry breathed out. "So, how are you enjoying yourself?"

"It's great. I'm currently in Prague," Emma informed her mother, her excitement causing her voice to come through high and chirpy.

Kerry smiled. The childlike awe with which her daughter spoke about her travels and the places she'd seen made Kerry wish that she was a kid again. Back then, her daughter had been in awe of everything and had promised she would never leave mommy's side.

"I'm happy you're enjoying yourself, sweetie."

"You should see this city now. It's so beautiful at night, the colors and the history. I feel like I could live here forever," Emma spoke contemplatively.

Kerry chuckled. "I'm sure you would."

"I'm serious, Mom," her daughter spoke up.

"I know you are, Emma," Kerry responded, a sad smile plastered on her lips. She knew more than anyone that once her daughter got it into her mind that she wanted to do something, she would do it with or without the support of anyone. She just hoped that even though she claimed to be serious, she didn't act upon it.

She didn't want to be in a situation where her child needed her, and she didn't know or just couldn't get to her in time because of the distance between them.

She couldn't go through something that debilitating again.

Chapter Six

"Our voices matter!"
"Our businesses matter!"
"We will not sell...We will not sell!"

Kerry stood out in the square of Downtown Oak Harbor with the other small business owners chanting as they staged their protest against Major Corp's plans to expand their reach on the island by buying out small businesses to build their high-rise structures and parking lots.

Many residents and tourists that were in town shopping, curious as to what was happening, drew nearer and stood by the pavement to watch them.

Kerry held up her placard that read, "Small businesses build community," matching what the other protesters were doing, holding up their own signs.

Ten minutes into the protest, the sound of a police siren was heard, and shortly after, it was pulled up at the curb. Two uniformed officers alighted from the car and headed their way.

"Good day, ladies and gentlemen. My name is Officer March, and this is my partner, Officer Blake. We're not here to sanction you, but we received a call that you were causing trouble for the businesses along this strip, that you're obstructing their customers."

"Officer, as you can see, we are in the quadrangle owned by the town and maintained by us taxpayers. How are we then in any way, shape, or form causing an obstruction?" Kerry asked, her tone serious.

The officers exchanged looks before the one who hadn't said anything before spoke. "We understand that but please just be mindful that if you obstruct people trying to get in and out of the business places, we will have to come back and break up your protest, peaceful or not," he warned.

"Thank you, Officers. We'll bear that in mind," Kerry responded with a tight-lipped smile.

"You folks have a good day now." The officers tipped their hats in farewell and returned to their squad car, and pulled off.

"Unbelievable," Kerry muttered under her breath. She turned to see the other protesters looking at her, uncertainty in their eyes, their signs hanging at their side.

"We have a right to protest what is happening to us. The police can't do anything because we aren't doing anything that isn't constitutionally allowed," she called out. "If it was enough for them to call the police, then that means they are paying attention, and our efforts aren't in vain. So, let's put that whole situation behind us and continue on," she implored.

Her fellow protesters nodded and murmured their agreement. Kerry raised her sign and her voice, "We deserve to be heard...our businesses matter." Soon more placards began going up, and there was a chorus of voices chanting for their rights. Satisfied with their response, she excused herself from making a call.

"Hey, Cousin. Did the journalist get there?" Cora greeted her when she picked up.

"That's what I was calling about, actually. I haven't seen her yet," she informed Cora.

"All right. Let me give her a call."

"Okay." With that, Kerry hung up and returned to the protest. Five minutes into it, she noticed the news van slowly coming down the street. When it parked, a woman with auburn hair pulled back in a tight bun at her nape and clothed in a burgundy skirt suit exited the van and walked over to the protesters. Kerry walked forward to meet her.

"Hi, you must be Faye Hunter," she greeted the woman, holding out her hand.

The woman took it while she adjusted her eyeglasses. "And you must be Kerry Hamilton-Johnson," she greeted.

"Just Kerry Hamilton," she corrected. "I don't go by Johnson anymore."

"Oh, not a problem," the woman replied. "So where can we conduct the interview?" she asked, looking at the protesters in the square and then back at her.

"How about the food court by the mall?" Kerry suggested.

The woman nodded contemplatively. "Sounds good," she finally agreed, allowing Kerry to lead the way. Kerry asked Anne to monitor the protest while she went to do the interview.

"So, what made you decide to have the protest," Faye asked, a notepad in her hand and her pen ready to add ink to paper recording Kerry's words.

"We realized... the other business owners and I realized that in order for the company to get the message that we wouldn't be selling our businesses and that we meant it, then protests were a good way to go. Plus, it seems they already have city hall in their po— by their side, so if we don't stand up for ourselves, no one else will."

The woman's head bobbed in understanding as she wrote on her pad.

"And why exactly are you against selling your businesses? From what I have gathered, the company is offering you all a hefty sum for these shops. You could even choose to set up somewhere else."

Kerry was stumped for a minute by the question. Sure, the money was good, and she could start another bakery, but it wouldn't be the same. "A fellow small business owner, Sylvie, her novelty store has been in her family for more than three generations. It provided jobs for a handful of unattached youth. She gave them a chance when no one else would, and they grew from it. The things her store sells are far more precious than what she could gain by selling her business. Mary-Ann has a beautiful flower shop just across from Sylvie. She grows and sells the most unique and exotic flowers, and her pottery is also well sought-after. You see, Faye, I could continue to tell you about the other owners, but what I want you to know is that our businesses are very important to the retention of all that makes Oak Harbor what it is. A large corporation takes away the community's identity, but we form personal relationships with the other business owners and our customers, which has a positive impact on the culture. It's like we become a close-knit family that is regularly welcoming new members to the club."

Faye's pen made frantic strokes across the paper as she tried to write all that Kerry had just said. Kerry decided to wait until she was finished with the tidbit she'd just given her to continue. When the woman looked up from her notes, she continued.

"You see, it isn't that we can't take the money and start over, but there are those to whom these businesses hold a deeper sentimental value than money. Plus, starting over again after having established yourself can be hard. To sum it up, we are a family right there at Midway Blvd and Goldie Road intersection, and that's how we want it to stay."

After the interview, Kerry thanked the woman for coming, and they exited the mall to rejoin the protesters and the woman to her news van that she had arrived in.

"So, how did it go?" Anne asked as they watched the reporter pull away from the curb, honking at them as she passed.

"It went...okay," Kerry replied.

"Just okay?" the older woman asked, folding her hands across her chest as she stared pointedly at Kerry.

Kerry shrugged. "I just spoke from my heart and my experience, so I guess we'll know how impactful it is when it is written."

"All right," Anne said, lips pursed.

Two hours after they had initiated the protest, it had finally ended with the protesters packing up their signs, getting into their cars, and driving away.

Kerry's phone rang just as she put the sign in the backseat of her car. Fishing it from her pocket, she started the call and held it to her ear.

"Hello?"

"Hey, it's me."

"Oh."

"You sound disappointed," Darren spoke observantly.

"Well, I can't say I'm especially thrilled," Kerry returned, getting into the driver's seat of her car.

"Touche."

Kerry rolled her eyes. "What is it that you want, Darren?"

"I called to find out if you could start helping me with my little situation today," he revealed.

Kerry released a defeated breath. She had planned to go home and catch up on some reading, but it seemed her plans were being derailed right now. At that moment, she wished she hadn't agreed to help him.

"I'm in the downtown area. I'll be there in five."

Fall is in the Air

"Thanks, Kerry. I owe you," her ex-husband praised.

"Don't you ever," she whispered to herself.

As she had promised, five minutes later, she was on an elevator up to the fourth floor where his suite of offices was.

"Good afternoon, Mrs. Johnson. Mr. Johnson is expecting you," the petite brunette seated around the desk stationed outside Darren's door informed her with a polite smile.

"Thank you, Irena," she replied, returning her smile. "And I just go by Hamilton."

"Okay," the woman who had been her ex-husband's secretary for the past five years replied.

Kerry walked past her desk and stood before the door. She knocked once and entered the office.

Darren was seated around a large oak desk, his brown hair tousled and his tie loosened. Stacks of paper covered the whole surface. Still, there were more boxes of paper all over the office. When he saw her, his hazel eyes lit up in relief. "I'm so glad you're here," he said with a wide smile.

Kerry's heart clenched at the action. It was a smile she hadn't received from him in more than eight years, but given the circumstances, she understood his reaction. Still, it caught her off guard, and her own reaction confused her.

Theirs had been more of a marriage of convenience after they hit the ten-year mark. They had remained together to ensure that their two girls remained in a stable home. They were just coexisting and co-parenting under the façade that everything was fine, but when the lights turned off and no one was around, they just couldn't stand to be in each other's space. Over time, the cracks just became too large to maintain, and when Sophia was in her senior year of high school, and Emma was in her sophomore year, the two decided to call it quits and get a divorce. Unbeknownst to them was the fact that the girls had anticipated it happening. They had thought they hid it so well, but the thing with cracks— they always leaked when it rained.

"It looks like a storm blew through here," she said, averting her gaze from the smiling man and stepping over a box, almost blocking the entrance. "Why are you so desperate to have this done discretely? What did you do?" she asked, finally reaching his desk to stare questioningly into his eyes.

"I didn't do anything wrong, Kerry." Darren sighed, falling into his chair with a defeated look.

Kerry scrunched up her brows in confusion. "Then why are you doing this?" she asked again.

Darren looked up at her. His eyes were tired-looking. "Someone has been siphoning funds from a few of our client's portfolios. I have an idea who it is, but I just need it confirmed before I can take any other actions," he spoke softly, but his tone was serious.

"Who?" she asked.

"I can't tell you that," Darren replied.

Kerry squinted as she looked at him. "If you want my help, then you'll have to trust me with everything. Otherwise, I'm walking out of here, and you can just find yourself another accountant," she threatened.

Darren glanced up at her, defiance in his hazel eyes with dark bags under them, indicating he probably had sleepless nights. Kerry stared back at him challengingly. Finally, Darren sighed and sat forward with his hands clasped, resting on his desk.

"Whatever I tell you cannot leave this room," he warned.

Kerry nodded in agreement.

After a long sigh, Darren said, "I think it's Mark."

Kerry widened her eyes as her mouth dropped open at the revelation. When she had recovered from the initial shock, she asked, "You mean...your best friend, Mark?"

Darren bobbed his head before looking over at the glass

panels that formed part of his wall giving a panoramic view of the city below.

Kerry folded her hands over her chest and paced back and forth in the small space that wasn't overrun with boxes. Finally, she stopped and looked at Darren with a serious expression.

"You realize my fees just went back up, right?"

Chapter Seven

Kerry yawned for the fourth time as she stood over the electric mixer whisking the wet and dry ingredients for the chocolate cake she was making. It had taken her three tries to measure out the correct amount of ingredients she needed.

"Boss lady. You look tired. Want me to take over?" Anne suggested, coming to stand beside her.

Kerry contemplated the offer. "Okay," she agreed, realizing that in her state, she might end up spoiling the batter and wasting resources. "I'm gonna go sit out at the front and maybe put my head down for a bit," she informed her second in command.

"Okay, you do that," Anne agreed, removing the mixing bowl from under the machine.

Kerry exited the kitchen. Looking over at the espresso machine at the far corner of the service area, she decided to make a cup of coffee. Hopefully, that could help wake her up and keep her going through the day.

She'd spent all yesterday afternoon cooped up in Darren's

office going over every single transaction the company had made in the past six months, looking for any discrepancies that could help them identify a pattern. They had managed to narrow it down to a few prominent portfolios that would have been difficult to identify that there was anything fishy going on unless you were actively looking. However, an external auditor would have spotted them. Even though they had identified the clients' portfolios that funds were being siphoned from, whoever was doing it was very clever as they didn't leave a paper trail. The funds had routed through multiple different accounts until they disappeared completely. They still hadn't found any indication that it had been transferred out to a Swiss account or any of the other private banks. Still, Kerry couldn't see why Mark would have done something like this. He and Darren had started the business from scratch and made it what it was today. They were the CEO and CFO. They didn't need to steal anything unless the company was in trouble. Something just wasn't adding up. In any case, she was sure that Darren had nothing to do with it. Despite their differences, she could vouch that he was a fair businessman and employer. They decided to call it quits just before daybreak, and Darren trailed her in his car until she was home.

Kerry took her cup of coffee and rounded the counter. She took a seat at one of the tables away from the window, her tired eyes still sensitive to the light. In the next hour, it would be time to open the bakery to their customers. She put her head down after a couple of sips of the hot, aromatic liquid. Needing to rest her eyes and relieve the pounding in her head, she folded her hands on the table and rested her head on them.

Kerry swatted away the annoying insect buzzing at her ear, but each time she thought she'd succeeded, it came back. In annoyance, she raised her head from the table, opening her eyes to look for the source of her irritation. As the cloud of confusion began to clear, she realized that the sound she was hearing was coming from the door. She looked over to see a man standing behind it. When he realized that he had gained her attention, he waved. She looked over at the clock behind the service counter and realized that it was ten minutes after the time the shop was supposed to be open.

Rising to her feet, she made her way over to the door to open up and let him in.

"Welcome to Heavenly Treats." She smiled at the gentleman. She couldn't recall ever seeing him in town.

"Thank you," he replied, cracking a smile of his own, his widening lips revealing perfectly even, white teeth. The corners of his light gray eyes crinkled with the movement, giving more life to his already striking face.

Kerry felt heat march up her neck, and she quickly averted her gaze from the stranger. She had to admit, he was a handsome gentleman, and he was well dressed too. He wore a trim-fit solid navy suit that fit flawlessly over his broad shoulders and teased at the muscular frame that lay under it without being too obvious.

"I want to apologize for earlier. We're usually open on time."

"It's fine. It happens to the best of us," he assured her, gracing her with another upturn of his lips.

She gave him a grateful grin. "What can I get for you?" she asked.

"A cup of what you're having would be nice," he replied, diverting his attention to the abandoned coffee cup on the table. She was sure it was probably tepid or acerbic by now.

"So that's one cup of fresh coffee. Would you like cream or sugar?"

"Yes. Both please," the man responded.

"Coming right up. Let me just get rid of this," she said, grabbing the cold coffee. She rounded the counter and poured it down the small sink by the expresso machine and disposed of the cup in the trashcan close by. She looked back at the man who was already staring intently at her. She gave him a small, pursed-lip smile, then turned to the espresso machine to escape the scrutiny of his eyes.

"Are you sure you don't want anything else?" she asked, glancing over her shoulder.

"No, I don't think so," he replied. "Unless..."

Kerry turned to look at him. "What's that?"

"Unless we can share it. I want to ask you about the town. I'm new here."

"Sure," Kerry replied. "Let me just inform my assistant pâtissier."

"Hey, Anne. When you're done, if it's not too much trouble, could you be at the front for about thirty minutes?"

"Sure thing," the woman replied, not bothering to lift her head from the cake she was decorating.

"Thanks," she said, heading to the front. "Okay, what do you want with your coffee?" she asked him.

The gentleman looked at the display case holding the baked goods. He thumbed his chin for some time before he finally responded. "I'll have two of your butter tarts," he ordered, looking back from the treats to her, his eyes dancing.

Kerry found herself smiling. "That's a great choice. You know they go well with strawberry syrup as well. Would you like some?"

"Sure," he replied with an easy grin.

Kerry fixed everything up, and after accepting payment, she closed the register and joined the man at the table he occupied.

"We didn't officially meet. My name is Ethan Sharpe," he introduced, holding his hand out to her.

"Kerry Hamilton," she returned, shaking the hand he offered. She noted that her hand fit well in his, enveloped hers like a glove. The warmth that traveled up her arm made her hyperaware, and she withdrew her hand, placing it in her lap.

"It's a pleasure to meet you," he said, smiling at her with his eyes. "And this is for you, for agreeing to sit with me." Ethan placed the dish with the butter tart before her.

"Thank you," she replied. "So, is this your first time here? In Oak Habor, I mean." Kerry took a bite of the sweet pastry and leaned back in the chair.

"Um yeah, yes, this is my first time here," Ethan replied, taking a sip of the coffee.

"And how has it been so far?"

"It's...it is a wonderful little town, quaint, but it's got a lot of potential," he replied.

Kerry nodded. "Business or pleasure?"

Ethan looked down and took a bite of his pastry. "I'm here on business," he replied before changing the subject. "So, what do you love about Oak Harbor? I'm assuming you are originally from here?"

"I am," Kerry affirmed. "Let's see. I love the fact that everyone knows almost everyone here. We are a close-knit town that thrives on the loyalty of the community. I like the fact that we have a lot of special landmarks that remind us so much of all that our ancestors went through to establish this town. I also love the fact that there are so many nature activities that are available such as hiking, sailing, whale watching, and bird watching...there's just so much to do and enjoy when you're here. That's the reason why outsiders visit all year round, and some of them even become a part of the fabric of our society."

"You are very passionate about this," the man observed, his lips slightly upturned. "It makes me want to experience these great activities myself."

"You should," Kerry spoke, leaning forward with her hands on the table, excited.

Ethan gave a soft chuckle at this, but then his face became

apologetic as he said, "Unfortunately, the business I'm here for won't allow me to do that."

"Okay. I'm sorry to hear that because I'm sure you would have enjoyed the activities, and who knows, maybe you wouldn't want to leave either."

"I'm sure I wouldn't," Ethan responded with a smirk.

Kerry gave him a small, shy smile.

At the sound of the bells chiming, Kerry slightly shook her head, not sure why she'd been staring at the man across from her, transfixed. She looked over at the front door to see the last person she would have expected to come into her bakery.

"Excuse me for a minute," she said to Ethan, who gave a slight nod of understanding.

Kerry rose to her feet and approached the man who stood by the door staring at Ethan as if he was public enemy number one. "What are you doing here, Darren? Just because I agreed to help you doesn't mean you just show up at my business whenever you feel like it. We're not friends, remember?" Kerry folded her hands across her chest as she waited for him to respond.

"Who's that?" Darren asked, still staring down at Ethan.

Kerry released a frustrated breath. "No one that should concern you. What do you want?"

Her ex-husband finally turned his gaze on her. "I think Mark suspects something is up."

"What did you say to him?" Kerry asked.

"Nothing really. Just that I couldn't go golfing with him this weekend because I have some paperwork I needed to go over, and then he asked what kind of paperwork and I couldn't find the right thing to say, and he offered to come to the office to help go over it, and I told him no, that I think he's done enough already..."

"Why would you say that?" Kerry looked at the man in disbelief.

"I don't know." Ethan sighed. "I guess I just panicked."

Kerry exhaled and put the heel of her right palm against her closed eyelid, trying to get rid of the tension headache she felt rising. "Look, Darren. You have to be more careful. These are serious allegations. You can't say anything about it unless you're absolutely sure."

"I know," the man replied solemnly.

"I'll try to come by the office later, but please...don't come here. We aren't at that level of amicability yet," she advised.

"Okay. You're right. I'll see you later." With one last look behind her, Darren left the bakery.

Releasing a long breath, Kerry turned to see Ethan on his phone. She hadn't meant to listen in on his conversation, but the bakery was small, and there weren't any other customers.

"I know, I told them I made the reservation last week, but they still don't see it, so now I have nowhere to stay for the duration of my time here...Yeah, I'll see if there are any bed-and-breakfasts I can stay at. Talk to you later."

Ethan smiled at her the moment he discontinued the call. "I hope I didn't do anything to upset your partner," he said apologetically.

"It's fine," Kerry waved it off. "He's my ex-husband."

"Oh," Ethan returned simply.

"Anyway, I sort of heard your conversation. I didn't mean to, but if you can't find a place to stay, my family owns an inn just fifteen minutes away from here. I'm sure they have space to accommodate you."

Ethan gave her a grateful grin. "That would be amazing. Thank you."

Kerry gave him an encouraging smile. "Will it be just you, or will your significant other be joining you?"

Ethan's face took on a faraway look. "It's just me... it's been that way for a number of years now," he replied simply. She nodded, not knowing what else to do.

"Let me just call the manager and then get you set up." Kerry fished her phone out of her pocket.

"Uh, Kerry...?"

She looked over at the man scratching the back of his head nervously.

"Before you do, I think there is something that I should let you know."

She gave him a quizzical look. "Okay?"

"I am an acquisitions lawyer, and Major Corp... they're my client."

Chapter Eight

Kerry looked at the man as if he'd just grown another head. She was completely floored by his revelation. It seemed Major Corp was really playing dirty to get what they wanted, using their employees to spy on the business owners to identify their weaknesses.

"You know, you really should have led with that statement at the beginning rather than tricking me to trust you like that," she said, a frown forming.

"I'm sorry, Kerry. It really wasn't my intention to deceive you, and if you realized, I didn't ask you anything about your business—"

"And that is supposed to make me what, grateful?"

"If I had said from the beginning that I was with Major Corp, would you have been this sociable to me?" he asked, coming to stand before her.

Kerry looked up into the gray eyes of the man standing over her, her own green ones filling with anger. "At the most, I would have remained civil and served you accordingly," she informed him.

"But you wouldn't have offered such good advice about the things that makes Oak Harbor such a great place."

She didn't say anything but just stood and looked at him with wary eyes.

Ethan sighed, running his hand along the corner of his head, smoothing back his brown curls. "I really am sorry if I came off as dishonest, but I truly just wanted to get to know you, know about this place so that I can make a fair judgment in this matter. I have to advise my clients whether or not the risk is worth it, and I also want to make sure that it's something that makes sense for the citizens as well."

Kerry felt her heart rate decrease a bit as her anger came down a notch. "But we've been saying it for months now. We don't want this," she spoke with feeling.

"I understand that, but the thing with acquisitions of this nature, we have to look at it on a long-term basis and no offense to you, but also the impact it will have on the town five— ten, even twenty years from now."

Her anger continued to dissipate, but instead of letting him see that, Kerry walked around the counter and started stacking the coffee cups and pastry containers to prepare for the morning rush that usually started an hour from opening time.

"I'm sorry, Kerry," she heard him repeat. "I'll just go."

Kerry turned to face him. "Where are you going?" she asked.

Ethan turned from the door with a look of confusion.

"Don't you need somewhere to stay?"

"Yeah, but—"

Kerry held up her hand to stop him. "You need somewhere to stay, and as much as I am annoyed by what you did, it would eat at me if you ended up staying in your car for the duration of your time here. We aren't like that in Oak Harbor. We might have our squabbles, but we still care."

"Okay," Ethan replied with a sigh of relief.

"Let me call the manager, and then I'll take you there if you can wait two more hours."

After confirming with Marg that there was space at the inn, Kerry instructed Ethan that he could go do what he needed to get done and meet her back at the bakery in two hours.

"That is one handsome man," Anne mused as they watched Ethan exit the bakery. "Pity he's working for that rattlesnake. You two could have made a nice couple."

Kerry whirled around to face the woman. "It doesn't matter if he was working for the pope. I still wouldn't be interested," she spat out. "I'm focusing on me and doing what I want. No man is going to come into my life and try to get me to conform to their ideals," she continued.

"Kerry," Anne spoke seriously, drawing her attention. "Not all men are the same. Take it from me. There is someone out there for everyone— you included, that will match your energy and do anything to ensure your happiness. Don't let what happened in your first marriage turn you off from finding something that could possibly transform your life."

Kerry nodded in understanding as she looked into the brown eyes of the woman whose wisdom shone through the fact that she had been on the earth longer than her and had suffered far worse than what she had.

"I'll try to be more open," she promised.

Two hours later, Ethan showed up. Kerry left with him trailing behind her in his blue Audi Q5. Fifteen minutes later, Kerry turned onto the path that was bordered by trees until she came to the semi-paved path fringed on either side by a plethora of low shrubs and flowers. Soon they arrived at the three-story colonial structure that was the inn.

Kerry parked along the side and waited for Ethan.

"Wow. This place is amazing," he spoke with awe as he came to stand beside her.

"It was owned by our great-grandfather four times removed

Fall is in the Air

and has been passed down from generation to generation. It was turned into an inn after the Civil War," Kerry said, giving him a history lesson as they made their way to the front. Soon they entered the great foyer topped off with a grand double staircase with a chandelier hanging pendulum style between them as the glass panels created an illusion of a cascading waterfall.

"Hi, welcome to the Willberry Inn. My name is Marg. You must be Ethan Sharpe." Marg held her hand out to Ethan with a bright smile on her lips.

"I am," he affirmed, taking her hand in a handshake.

"It's lovely to have you, and I hope that while you're here, you'll enjoy all the amenities that are available to you as our guest."

"Thank you."

Marg gave him a slight nod of acknowledgment before turning to Kerry.

"Hi, Kerry. It's so good to see you," she said, giving her a friendly hug.

"It's good to see you too, Marg. I hope my cousin hasn't been a bother to you."

"Oh, not at all. Quite the contrary. Ben is wonderful."

Kerry grinned in satisfaction at the telltale blush the woman sported as she spoke about Ben. "Well, I gotta get going now, but it was good seeing you, Marg. We'll catch up on girls' night."

"Yes, we will," Marg agreed.

Kerry turned to Ethan. "Now that I've gotten you somewhere to stay for the duration of your visit to Oak Harbor, I hope you'll get to feel the true authenticity of this place," she told him.

"There is no doubt that I will," he returned with a smile. "Thanks again.

Kerry turned and made her way to her car. She decided to

go visit her aunt instead of heading immediately back to the bakery. When she got to the house, she noted that her father's car was also there. After parking her vehicle, she went up the stairs and rang the doorbell. None other than Luke answered the door.

"Hey, baby girl," the man greeted with a small smile.

"Hi, Dad," she greeted back with a small upturn of her own lips.

"Did you come to visit the girls?" he asked.

"Um, not actually. I came to visit with Aunt Becky," she informed him. "Is Mom here as well?"

"No, she stayed back to get some housework done," Luke informed her. He stepped away from the door and allowed her inside.

"Look, Kerry. I know that we won't see eye to eye on many things, and I still think you're making a mistake hanging on to that business, but can we at least try to get back to the relationship we had?"

Kerry folded her hands over her chest and stared at him seriously. "How can we when you keep saying things like this, Dad? You want us to rebuild our relationship, but you try to ridicule and put down the choices I made with every single opportunity you get."

"That's not true," Luke defended.

"Isn't it?" she countered.

Luke sighed, running his hand over his hair. "I'm sorry that's the way you see it, sweetie, but I really just want what's best for you."

"If you want what's best for me, Dad, you'll leave me to make my own choices," she replied, with her hands over her chest.

Luke held up his hands. "Okay, I hear you. I'll try," he said.

"Thanks, Dad. I'm just gonna go see Aunt Becky now."

Fall is in the Air

Kerry placed a small kiss against her father's cheek and headed for the back.

She found Becky seated on the rocking chair, looking out toward the harbor.

"Penny for your thoughts?"

Becky's head turned to her with a look of surprise and pleasure. "Kerry, it's so good to see you. How are you doing?"

"I'm fine, Aunt Becky," she replied, leaning down to accept the hug from the woman's open arms. She noted that they shook slightly, and it seemed her aunt couldn't hold them up for long. She hated the fact that she was battling such a debilitating and deadly illness. If only there was a way to reverse the effects. Still, she was happy that even with ALS, the support of the family had kept the disease from getting worse for a little longer.

"How is the bakery?" Becky asked as soon as Kerry took a seat in the chair opposite her.

"It's great. I have increased the number of customers in the last three months, and it seems to be on the right trajectory," she informed her aunt.

"But?" Becky asked, sensing that something was still wrong.

Kerry blew out a breath. "Between the company trying to buy it and Dad's lack of support, I just feel so discouraged at times," she confessed.

She felt her aunt's hand reach over and grasp hers, slight tremors from her causing Kerry's hand to shake as well. She looked over to see her aunt grinning at her with reassurance.

"All will be well, Kerry. You are a fighter, and I know that there is no way you're allowing them to take away something you've worked so hard for. You'll make them see that the bakery is worth it where it's located."

Kerry smiled in gratitude at her aunt.

"Your father, like my Samuel, is set in his ways. They believe in protecting their families the way they see fit, and sometimes they just don't understand that what they're doing is not the way to go about it. Sam realized in the end, but then it was too late."

The woman's face took on a look of melancholy, and it was Kerry's time to offer some support. She squeezed her hand to remind her that she, too, was not alone.

Becky looked over and beamed at her niece. "Your father is a family man, Kerry. He loves his family with his whole life, so I know that with time and with you both talking about what's happening, it will get better, and your bond will be strengthened to become stronger than ever."

Kerry gave the woman a look of gratitude before turning to look out at the Harbor. She hoped that was the truth.

Chapter Nine

"Good morning."

"Hi. You're here?"

"Yup."

"Talking to me?" Ethan pointed to himself before looking behind him as if expecting there to be someone else there in the inn's foyer.

Kerry chuckled at his actions. "I get that I came off a little strong and defensive yesterday. That's on me. It's just that I'm very passionate about the things that mean something to me," she informed him.

Ethan nodded in understanding. "Why did you come to call on me, though?" he asked, his voice still laced with confusion.

"I came to see if you're free to go visit some of the sites of attraction that Oak Harbor has to offer," she responded in a hopeful tone.

Ethan widened his eyes in surprise.

"I know you said you would be busy for the duration of your time here trying to take over the world for 'Major Corp' and all." She made air quotes with her fingers at the latter part of her statement as she tried hard not to roll her eyes with disdain.

Noticing the crease in his forehead from where his brows drew together and his lips tightening as his jaw tensed, Kerry held up her hand in concession, fixing her face in the most apologetic look she could muster. "That was uncalled for. I'm sorry."

Ethan gave a slight nod, but his annoyed expression didn't ease much.

"Back to why I'm really here," she rushed out. "Again, I know you're super busy, but I really want to take you out, not like on a date or anything, but just so you'll get a feel of the island and its environment. I really believe that it will help you to make the right decision."

"And what decision might that be?" Ethan asked, hands crossed over his chest as he stared at her.

"That...um," Kerry turned away from him, having lost her train of thoughts as his steel-gray eyes stared at her as if searching her very soul. "I believe that you'll come to realize that Major Corp building here would be a huge mistake and that you'll tell them exactly that," she responded, compelling herself to stare into his eyes and not be bothered as she delivered her speech.

A moment of silence passed between the two as they stood still, staring back at each other. Ethan broke that silence as he burst into a low, deep laugh that vibrated his whole chest.

"You're very bold," he said when he'd settled down.

"So, I've been told," she returned with a bright smile.

Ethan stared at her for a few more seconds, his expression unreadable. Kerry wondered what was going through that head of his. She really wanted him to say yes to her proposition because she believed that if he got to see the town in a different way, the way the citizens and even tourists got to view it, he'd be on her side— that it was fine just the way it was and needed no additions.

"Let's say I agree to go on this excursion with you. What are we talking here?" The evenness of his tone revealed nothing. She couldn't tell if he was considering it or just humoring her.

"Well...first, I would take you hiking at one of my favorite spots and see where it takes us from there."

Ethan held his chin between his index and thumb, his eyes contemplative.

"That means we'd have to leave here shortly so that we can beat the morning sun," she added when he still hadn't spoken.

Finally, Ethan looked back at her. "Okay," he replied simply.

"Okay, as in you're in?" she asked slowly.

Ethan broke out into a bright smile that caused her heart to skip a beat. "It means yes. I will allow you to show me around town and all it has to offer, but I'm not making any promises that it will affect my decision at all."

"Of course," Kerry accepted his caution, a grin broadening her lips.

"I have to be back before three, though. I have a conference call at that time," he informed her.

"All right, I'll have you back long before that and in one piece." She smirked.

Ethan chortled. "Fine. Let me change into something more suitable," he said, looking down at the baggy rugby shirt he wore over a pair of jeans.

"I'll be waiting," Kerry promised. She watched him as he turned and took the stairs two at a time, his long strides taking him half the time to make it to the second floor. Ten minutes later, he was back in the foyer dressed in gray slacks and a blue polo shirt, and sneakers.

"Ready to go?" he asked once he was standing before her.

"Yes, I am," she replied, heading toward the exit.

"Why don't you ride in my car? It'll save on fuel and give us some more time to talk," Ethan suggested.

Kerry paused to think about it. "Sure," she replied with a smile.

Ethan returned her smile before directing her to his car. Pressing the key fob, he unlocked the car and opened the door for her. She thanked him before settling against the plush leather seat, reveling in how comfortable it felt.

Shortly after, Ethan rounded the car to settle in the driver's seat beside her. They pulled out of the driveway and followed the pathway until they emerged from a wooded area, shrouding the property from visibility, and headed down the highway.

"Turn right," Kerry instructed a few minutes later, directing him to turn on State Route 20E. "This is Skagit County, home to the best and most exotic species of tulips this side of the pond," she informed him when she noticed him staring out at the copious rows of raised plant beds.

Ethan glanced over at her with raised brows.

"During the fall, the horticulturists plant the bulbs in the rows just in time for the first frost. This ensures that they bloom by late March or early April just in time for the Tulip festival."

"Sounds interesting," he responded, nodding thoughtfully as he stared at the road again.

"It is," she replied. "Every year, over a million visitors visit the island for this festival and the annual art exhibition back in Oak Harbor. Did you know that we have two very famous artists that call the island home?"

"No, I didn't," Ethan responded, glancing sideways at her before focusing his gaze on the road.

"We do," she said proudly. "That's the Olympic Mountain Range." She directed his gaze to the sprawling, dark landmass with snowcapped summits. "In winter, most of the mountain face is covered with snow, and we can go skiing, same with the cascades mountains which are to the north."

Ethan nodded as he listened.

"It looks like I'm boring you," she spoke reticently.

Ethan briskly shook his head no. "Not at all. I'm enjoying your voice," he responded.

Kerry widened her eyes in surprise at this revelation, and her heart skipped a beat.

"I mean, I enjoy the facts that you're presenting from a place of knowledge and how passionate you are about this," he rushed on to say.

Kerry smiled sheepishly and looked forward. "We're almost there," she spoke lightly, hoping to dispel the awkward tension that had surfaced from his comment.

"Where exactly is there?" he asked, briefly glancing at her before turning his gaze forward again.

"Bowman Bay, it's another section of Deception Pass State Park," she responded. "It's a great place to show you the magic of this place."

Two minutes later, they were exiting the car at the designated parking lot. After paying for the park pass at the kiosk, Kerry led Ethan toward the dirt path bordered by wood fences leading down to the shoreline of the bay.

"Wow! You weren't kidding about the charm of this place," Ethan awed as he stood beside her, looking out at the view before him. The vast green waters roared as the waves rolled over each other, rushing for the shore and crashing against the coarse black sand, moving the particles laterally up and down the shoreline at the ebb and flow of the tide. The clear blue skies above the uniform green of the land masses protruding from the water's edge formed the perfect backdrop for a holiday postcard.

"You haven't seen anything yet." Kerry smirked. She walked along the shoreline, and Ethan followed. She led him across the small wooden bridge that transitioned to a marked dirt path. The path led through a forest of evergreens that arched over the path creating a canopy of leaves and limiting the light reaching the forest floor.

"Have you ever been hiking?" Kerry asked as the path grew steeper.

"It's been a few years since I last did that," Ethan spoke from behind her.

"I'll go easy on you then," she turned to advise him, a grin on her lips.

"Don't hold back. I'll keep up," he assured her.

"You sure?" she asked with a quirked brow.

"Very sure," Ethan replied, a confident smile on his lips and a glint in his eyes.

"Okay," she returned, her smile growing broader at the perceived challenge. She turned and began picking her way along the path, allowing adrenaline to propel her forward as she stepped over fallen tree trunks and found secure footing from protruding rocks to haul herself over.

"How are you doing?" she twisted to ask.

"Great," Ethan replied, face glowing with sweat.

Kerry was impressed. For someone who had mentioned he didn't have much time to do the outdoorsy activities and such, he was surely holding his own and keeping up with her pace, and she hadn't held back. She wasn't boasting or anything, but she prided herself in maintaining her athleticism. She did it all, from hiking to kayaking to paragliding and so many more energy-packed activities.

"I hit the gym at least four times a week for an hour or so," Ethan spoke up, answering her unasked question. "I have to ensure that I maintain my figure," he continued, flexing playfully.

Kerry laughed at his silliness. "Come on, there's somewhere

I need to show you," she directed, turning to start the trek again.

About two minutes later, they turned left where the foliage began to thin until they came to a clearing. It led to the edge of the mountain and gave a bird's eye view of the Deception Pass Bridge. The gargantuan wrought iron structure stood tall and regal as it ran through the elevated landforms as if it was borne out of an act of nature's will to connect the two small islands.

"This is amazing," she heard him breathe out beside her. It brought a triumphant smile to her lips.

"I told you, you would fall in love with this place," she spoke knowingly.

"You did," Ethan affirmed, turning to grace her with the upturn of his lips, a small depression forming in his left cheek just below his gleaming eyes.

Kerry averted her gaze to look out across the pass, confused as to why the appearance of his dimple caused her breath to catch in her chest.

"So, have I convinced you even a little bit to consider telling your clients to go sho...to withdraw their offer?" she asked, looking up at him with guarded eyes.

Ethan let out a throaty chuckle before turning to look at her, his gray eyes twinkling. "As much as I enjoyed doing this with you...honestly, I'm not convinced that the area is not a lucrative spot for the plaza they're planning to build. In trajectory, their business will bring a lot of exposure to the island and help with brain drain..."

Kerry sighed in exasperation. "I take it they have a pamphlet that you get to recite those words from," she spoke sullenly as she turned her gaze back to looking out at the water.

"I'm sorry that I don't have the words that you want to hear," Ethan responded after more than a minute of silence. "But my job is to offer the best advice to my client, and currently, what I said, whether it's from a pamphlet or not, is the best option for them."

"I'm sorry, Ethan, I shouldn't have said that. I was just disappointed. It's not your fault. I shouldn't have taken it out on you," Kerry said apologetically.

"It's fine. I get it," Ethan assured her, smiling.

The two didn't speak much after that as they made their way back to the park's entrance. A half hour later, they were back on the highway, and fifteen minutes later, they turned onto NE Regatta, then onto Torpedo Road, and shortly after, they turned at the sign welcoming them to the Willberry Inn and restaurant.

"I'm sorry if I put a wrench in your plans," Ethan apologized after parking his car and walking Kerry to hers.

"It's okay," she replied. "It just means I have to work harder to convince you," she continued, a small but confident smile lifting the corners of her mouth.

"That feels like a challenge." Ethan smirked.

"Take it however you choose to." She returned his smirk.

"All right then. Challenge accepted." His smile grew even broader.

Kerry looked down to see his hand extended, and she eagerly took it, ignoring the warmth that traveled from where their skin connected up her arm. "Challenge accepted," she repeated. And she would win. There was no way she would allow this to be added to the list of mistakes she'd made. She had to win.

Chapter Ten

Kerry ran her hands over the smooth, velvety petals of the tulips in full bloom, taking in the colorful flowers that stretched as far as her eyes could see. She especially loved the way they seemed to dance with the slight breeze that whooshed over them, carrying with it their light honey infused with a spicy aromatic scent across the landscape. She bent to take in a bigger whiff of the scent, a smile of contentment broadening her lips.

"What are you doing?"

Kerry jumped up, surprised that someone else was in the fields with her. Turning around, she saw a young woman some distance away. She could tell that she was young just by the symmetry of her slim body and by the way she dressed in mid-thigh denim shorts, frayed at the ends, and a blouse that nearly covered the shorts. She couldn't see her face no matter how hard she tried, but she had a distinct feeling that she knew her.

"I'm sorry, I thought I was alone," she said by way of answer as the young woman stood with her arms crossed over her chest, waiting.

The girl scoffed. Kerry's head jerked back slightly in surprise.

"I'm sorry, did I do something wrong?" she asked, looking around uncomfortably. "I can go."

"Did you do something wrong?" the young woman sneered.

Kerry arched her brow in confusion. She wasn't sure what the cause was, but it was obvious the young woman was angry with her.

"Do...do I know you?" she asked, her hand crossed over her heart.

Slowly, the woman's hands dropped to her sides as her shoulders slumped. "No," she replied sadly. "You don't."

This left Kerry even more confused. "Then why are you s—"

"The reason you don't know me is because you never took a chance to get to know me," the woman interrupted, her words infused with angry accusation.

Kerry furrowed her brows at the whiplash from the girl's words. "I'm sorry. What is this about?" she asked, frustrated.

"It's about how the one person I should be able to depend on in the whole wide world decided that I wasn't worth the trouble and abandoned me to an unknown fate," the woman spoke calmly.

Again, Kerry furrowed her brows, but as she processed the words, her eyes slowly widened with realization, and her hand came up over her mouth in shock.

"Got your attention now, didn't I?" the woman smirked.

"You're...y-you're my daughter," she breathed out shakily.

"Congrats, MOM." The woman clapped before her as if Kerry had just won a prize.

"I can't believe this...but...but how are you here?" Kerry asked, lifting her hand to reach for the young woman but letting it fall by her side helplessly.

"Don't worry, I'm just a figment of your guilty conscience," she replied. Kerry could hear the smile in her speech, but she still couldn't see her face.

"Why won't you let me see you?" Kerry asked softly, with her hands up, pleading.

"Why should I? I have been faceless to you for the past twenty-three years. Why should I let you see me now? Is it to heal your guilt?"

"I just need to see you, sweetheart," Kerry pleaded as tears fell down her face.

"You shouldn't have given me up for adoption, Mom. I wouldn't have been a nameless, faceless person in your dreams."

"Baby, I am truly sorry. I shouldn't have given you up, but you don't understand, I didn't have a choice—"

"You always have a choice," the woman shouted, halting Kerry's pleading. "You had the choice to keep me, to fight for me, and you didn't. Now, you'll never know what I look like, what my laughter sounds like, what my dreams and aspirations are...you don't even know how I fared after being adopted. Do you know why? Because you chose *you* and not me."

Kerry woke with a start. She placed her hands over her cheeks, feeling the wetness on her fingertips. She hadn't had a dream like that in years. It felt as if her heart was being ripped out as the weight of regret lodged in her chest. She burst into uncontrollable sobs, covering her mouth with her hands to stem the sound. When the tears had subsided, she pulled back the covers and swung her legs over the side of the bed as she spread her arms wide, flattening her palms against the foam mattress for support. She leaned forward with her eyes closed.

Kerry remained in the same position for a few more minutes before pushing herself up and walking over to her closet. Sliding one of the glass panels to the side, she entered the sizeable room packed with rows and rows of outfits, shoes, and purses, some of which she hadn't even worn yet. Give her a pair of jeans and a white T-shirt, and she was fine. She wasn't that interested in dressing up unless it was to go on a girls' night out. However, none of those were the reasons for her being in the closet at 3:00 a.m. She reached for the short step ladder and positioned it below one of the high shelves. After stepping up, she reached up and felt all the way to the back of the shelf until her fingers brushed against the object of interest. Carefully, she brought down the small wooden, heart-shaped chest, wiping off the slight dust resting on it for not being handled in a long time.

She brought the box to her room and sat on the bed while she looked down at it on her lap. After a few hesitant tries, she finally inserted the key she kept on her bedside table into the small opening in the box. She gingerly lifted the lid to look down at the contents it had been protecting. Gently, she pulled out the small pair of wooly baby socks and rubbed them against her cheek with a small, sad smile. Next was a hospital wristband marked for the maternity ward and had her name on it. She ran her fingers over the writing before putting it back into the box.

Kerry reached for the small jewelry box in the corner of the chest. Slowly, she opened it and reached for the locket secured on a single, thin gold chain. She ran her fingers over the inscription "SJ" for Sara Jessica— the name she had planned to give to her daughter. She fumbled with the locket latch, trying to get it open, but her hands shook so much that she had to take a minute to collect herself and take deep, calming breaths. Finally, she managed to open the locket.

Kerry felt the breath leave her body in rapid, uneven gasps as her eyes focused on the small photo contained in the locket. It was a photo of a young baby wrapped in a receiver with a pink tam on her head. She hugged the locket tightly against her chest as a deluge of tears rushed down her face and splashed against her hands.

"I'm so sorry," she sobbed. "I should have done more. I should have fought for you. I'm so, so sorry."

As she sobbed for her child and for her mistake, her mind unwillingly transported her to the chain of events that had ended with her giving away her daughter.

"What are your plans?"

"I don't know," a young Kerry replied timidly. She truly didn't know what to do. She was glad that her father had come for her, but now that he was there and she got to experience the disappointment with which he spoke to her or whenever he chose to look at her, that she saw in his eyes, she kind of wished she had chosen to take it all on by herself.

"Kerry, you have to have a plan." Her father sighed.

She wrapped her hands over the top of her protruding stomach, feeling helpless and confused.

"Do you plan to raise this baby on your own, or will you pressure the father to become involved in this? Are you planning to go back to school? Will you be working as you try to support yourself and your baby? These are questions you have to consider, Kerry," her father rattled off as he paced the small space between her bed and the front door.

"I didn't think—"

"That's it. You didn't think, and now you have no plan on how to get yourself out of this mess. Your mother and I were so worried about you, Kerry. Did you consider how your actions affected us?" Her father finally said what he had been holding back since getting to Dallas two days ago. She knew it was coming, had braced herself for it. It didn't make it any easier to take it, though. Her father's speech made her feel lower than low, as if she was nothing but a disappointment to her family.

"I'm so sorry, Daddy," she replied, gulping back her tears and the lump in her throat. "I didn't mean to hurt you or Mom."

She heard her father sigh before he walked over to where she stood and brought her into his chest as he hugged her. Luke placed a small kiss against her temple.

"I know, sweetheart," he replied in a tired, defeated voice above her head. "I know. As much as I love you and wish I could make every decision for you, you've proven what the outcome would have been."

"What can I do to prove that I am sorry for what I did?" Kerry asked, staring up at her father with pleading green eyes. "Please, Daddy," she begged when no response came.

Luke looked down at his daughter, his sharp blue eyes serious. "Do you think you have what it takes to take care of this child?" he asked calmly.

Kerry separated from him as she thought about the question. Was she capable of taking care of a child all by herself? How would having a child affect her chances of pursuing her goals? Her mind shifted to Mark, who was out there having a jolly good time and probably picking up a girl in every state he visited. She thought about how easy his life was. How quickly he had rejected their child growing inside her and how much she wasn't able to divorce herself from the situation as he had. When she thought about it, she was the only person that was all in.

She thought about how selfish it would be for her to expect her parents to raise her child for her while she went back to school. They had a plan, and she had chosen to go against it. It would be unfair of her to impose such a responsibility on them that was solely born out of her stubbornness and stupidity.

She was just a little over a month away from delivery, and she hadn't bought more than a few pieces of baby clothing. As she thought about her father's question, the truth blatantly stared her in the face and caused her shoulders to droop.

"No, I don't have what it takes to care for my baby," she replied, hanging her head. Her father brought her close once more in comfort.

Fall is in the Air

One month later, Kerry gave birth to a beautiful, healthy baby girl, and two days later, she no longer belonged to Kerry.

Kerry snapped out of her reverie, shaking her head in melancholy. She should have fought harder to keep her daughter. She should have done more.

She brought the locket to her chest once more as the tears meandered their way down her cheek.

"I will do right by you," she promised, rubbing her hands over the indentations of the inscriptions on the locket.

Chapter Eleven

Kerry pulled into the driveway of her parents' house and made her way toward the porch and the front door. The door swung open less than a minute after she rang the bell.

"Hi, Mom," she greeted the woman who stared up at her in surprise.

"I'm happy to see you, but I never expected to see you back in this house until at least a month has passed, but here you are. Two visits in a week and a half," her mother marveled as she stepped to the side to give her daughter entry to the house.

"You make it sound like I choose not to come over on purpose, Mom," Kerry replied, slightly offended.

"I'm sorry, honey. I didn't mean for it to sound that way. I am truly happy that you're here this evening," the woman responded.

Kerry gave her a tightlipped smile as she willed herself to hold back the snide comment just on the tip of her tongue. "Is Dad here?" she asked, changing the subject.

"He's out by the back porch catching up on the news."

Fall is in the Air

Kerry quirked her brow in question.

"He still has that little portable radio from back when you were eight," Maria informed her.

"Really? It still works?" She laughed in disbelief.

"It does. He gets a number of stations on it too," her mother confirmed. "Are you staying for dinner?" she asked the minute they entered the kitchen.

"Yes, I am," Kerry answered.

"Oh good." Maria grinned. "I made the lasagna casserole in the larger oven pan, but none of the others are coming over. That means I would have to refrigerate the rest for some other time," she explained after seeing Kerry's expression. "Now that you're here, we only have to put back half."

Kerry chuckled at her mother's logic. "Need help?" she asked as she watched her get on her tippy-toes to try to reach the dishes high up in the cupboard. Her mother looked over her shoulder briefly before turning and continuing with what she was doing.

Kerry walked over to where her mother stood and reached over her to take down the dishes the woman had been struggling to reach.

"Thank you," she responded. Kerry followed her to the dining room.

"Kerry, you're here," her father's surprised voice reached her ears.

"I am," she replied with a small smirk that looked more like a grimace. "I was telling Mom that I was in the neighborhood, and since she's always berating me for not showing up here more often, I decided to come and have dinner with my two lovely parents."

"Okay," Luke replied, giving her a weird look. "Are you sure you're okay?" he asked.

"Never better," she replied, plastering a bright smile on her face.

Ten minutes later, they were seated around the table, enjoying Maria's lasagna. "I made the noodles from scratch," she told Kerry, who was enjoying the consistency of the lasagna. "I made the sauce from tomato puree with oregano and parsley and topped it with feta cheese."

"It's really good, Mom," Kerry complimented.

"Thank you, dear," her mother responded, pleased.

Luke dabbed at his mouth with the napkin and placed it on the table before turning curious blue eyes on Kerry. "So, sweetheart, is there anything that you want to tell us?"

Kerry looked away from her mother to her father with a small, reserved smile on her lips and guarded eyes. "Not that I can recall, Dad," she replied simply.

Luke inclined his head in acknowledgment before reaching for the dish to scoop out another serving of the lasagna.

"Actually...that's not true."

Luke paused midway to look at her.

"I've decided that I want to look for my daughter," she finished, turning her head back to her meal as if she hadn't just dropped a bomb at the table.

"Who, Emma?" Luke asked, with his brows scrunched together. "She'll be fine. You already gave her the go-ahead to travel the world, and that's exactly what she's doing. I'm sure she'll be home soon and when this phase is over so that she can focus on the important things like college and starting a career. She's currently living out her adventurous years just like her mother."

Kerry shook her head as a small chuckle of disbelief rocked her chest. She set her gaze on her father as she asked, "And what if she gets pregnant, hmm? Should I attribute it to her having the same wild, irresponsible side that I have? Should I then force her to give up the baby too?"

The table fell silent. The tension was so thick it could be cut with a knife.

"Where is all this coming from, Kerry?" her father asked, his voice serious.

Kerry stared from her father to her mother and back. "I want to find my daughter... the one I gave up for adoption."

Her parents stared gobsmacked at her.

"How do you plan to find her?" her father asked. He stared at her, folding his arms across his chest, waiting for a response. "You wouldn't know where to start looking," he concluded as she sat before him, unspeaking.

Kerry stared at her father as her brain worked hard to come up with the answer. "I'll start where it all began— the hospital."

"That's impossible," her father threw back at her.

"No, it's not."

"It was a closed adoption which means the records are confidential, Kerry."

It was Kerry's time to fold her hands over her chest as she contemplated his words. "It doesn't mean it's impossible. It just means that I have to use a little bit more resources to find her," she articulated.

Luke shook his head as he fixed her with a disconcerted look. "So, you're willing to do whatever it takes to find the young woman, and then what? Are you willing to disrupt her life given that she probably doesn't know that she is adopted to satisfy your own selfish desires?"

"At least it will be my decision this time," she griped, a wave of frustration washing over her.

"What's that supposed to mean?" Luke threw back at her, the gruffness in his voice telling.

"All right, that is enough," Maria spoke up, rising from her seat to look at her husband and her daughter, her hazel eyes full of annoyance.

"We are at the dining table, for God's sakes. Can't you two put aside your differences for five minutes so that we can have a nice family meal together?"

"I'm sorry, sweetheart, you're right," Luke appeased his wife. "We'll finish the conversation after dinner." He looked to his daughter for confirmation.

"Yeah, Mom, I'm sorry about that," she responded apologetically.

"Good," her mother replied, satisfied. Maria lowered herself back into her seat, and the meal continued, the trio carrying out a lighter conversation.

After dinner, Kerry chose to head home and avoid further confrontation with her father.

"I've got to go, Mom. Dinner was superb," she complimented with a smile after helping her clear the table.

"Okay, sweetie, be safe on your way home. Whatever you decide to do, I promise I will support you."

Kerry gave her mother a grateful smile as she accepted her hug. "Thanks, Mom. I appreciate that."

"I love you, sweetie," Maria spoke against her daughter's ear as she held her tighter as if afraid she would lose her if she let her go. "All I have ever wanted is for you to be happy."

Kerry pulled away from the embrace and gave her mother a small smile. "I've gotta run. Can you tell Dad I'll speak to him later, maybe?"

"Sure, sweetheart. I'll let him know," Maria replied, giving her a closed-lip smile. She reached up to rest her palm against her daughter's hair, lovingly smoothing it back. "I'm happy you came."

Kerry gave her mother a closed-lip smile of her own. "I'll talk to you later, Mom." With that, Kerry turned and walked out of the kitchen and toward the foyer. She made it to the front door and reached to turn the doorknob.

"So you're leaving without saying anything to me? Is that how it'll be every time there's an issue?"

Her father's words stopped her actions, and she whirled to

face him. Kerry sighed as she stared up at her father standing by the staircase with his arms folded across his chest, his expression unreadable. "Look, Dad. I know we'll never see eye to eye, and I know that you don't agree with the decisions I make most of the time, but that's just the thing... they're my decisions," she told him.

"I gather that means your mind is made up, and you'll be looking for that young woman," he concluded.

Kerry shrugged as she gave a tactful response, "Again, Dad, it is my decision, whatever it may be, even if you don't agree with it."

"And what about the girls, the two daughters that you've grown that know nothing about that part of your past? What will you tell them?" he asked.

"I'll worry about that when the time comes. Sophia and Emma will understand," she responded, not sure if it was her father she was trying to convince of this or herself. "Look, Dad. I gotta go. I've got some things to do before I head home," she explained.

"Okay, sweetheart," her father replied. His hands fell to his side as he made eye contact with her. Kerry saw a myriad of emotions flash through his sapphire blue irises before settling on concern. "I love you," he spoke before turning and heading for the kitchen.

"I love you too, Dad," Kerry whispered dejectedly as she watched him disappear from sight. She turned and pulled the front door open, welcoming the darkness enveloping her in a shroud of uncertainty.

Instead of heading in the direction of home, she directed her car in the direction of downtown. She needed to take her mind off everything that just happened, even if for a short while. She wanted to find her daughter. She wanted to know that she was okay. Maybe it was a little selfish, but after the dream she had, she couldn't knock the feeling that this was something she needed to do— as if her daughter needed her to find her.

Ten minutes later, all of which seemed a blur with the loudness of her thoughts, she was outside Darren's building. She made her way to the lobby, giving the front desk security a slight nod in greeting. She got to the elevator and stepped inside. Pressing the fourth floor, she rested her head against the cold steel wall as she waited for it to make the short journey up. In less than ten seconds, the doors dinged open. She removed her face from the wall and walked through the doors. The office was quiet as the staff had left for the day. Darren's receptionist wasn't at her desk, which was cleared of personal items, but she could see light coming from under the office door. She walked up to it and knocked.

A minute later, it opened to reveal a disheveled Darren staring back at her in surprise. "I wasn't expecting you here today."

Kerry gave him a tight-lipped smile. "Well, hello to you too, Darren. How nice of you to open the door for me."

Darren scratched the back of his head. "I'm sorry about that. I just thought that you would call whenever you were stopping by," he explained.

"Why are you having another meeting? Is someone else here, a mystery woman perhaps?" she asked with a knowing smile, trying to look past Darren into his office.

"What? Of course not," the man replied in a slightly offended voice. "It's just me here. I was going through the last set of transactions." He moved aside to give her access.

"Relax, I was just messing with you," she replied, walking past him to see the office still in a chaotic state.

Darren turned to her with furrowed brows. "Are you all right?" he asked, watching her as she walked around the office.

Kerry turned to look at her ex-husband, her vulnerability evident. She turned back to the glass-paneled wall.

Fall is in the Air

"Kerry, what's wrong?"

She slowly turned to the man staring at her with concern. Her face felt wet. She reached up to swipe under her eye with her index finger.

"Kerry," Darren repeated cautiously.

She turned her now blurry vision on the man standing rigidly by the door as he stared back at her.

"I need to find my daughter."

Chapter Twelve

Kerry sat by the counter mindlessly stirring the cup of coffee that she'd been sipping for the past half hour. She stared into the murky liquid so reflective of her current mood. She had met a dead end, calling the hospital back in Texas. She had been transferred to several departments until her call was escalated to the chief physician, who had been adamant that there was nothing that could be done as the records were completely sealed and there was no way to get in contact with the parents as the case was treated as a phantom adoption. In a nutshell, there was no way that they would release information to her. She'd expected that but having it confirmed left her feeling despondent. She was relieved that she had given Anne the day off as she knew the perceptive woman would have picked up that she wasn't at her best. She just wasn't in the mood to talk.

Kerry's head felt as if a ton of bricks were resting on top of it. She pushed the cup of coffee away and rested her head against her folded arms on the counter. She breathed heavily as her mind ran on. The life she'd lived thus far flashed before her.

She pondered the choices she made that led to her current position. She couldn't deny the life that she had now. She had two lovely daughters who she loved to bits, a loving family that she was able to depend on despite the conflicts that arose from time to time, and she had a business that she loved. But she wondered how her life would have turned out if she had chosen to keep her daughter all those years ago. How would it have affected the trajectory of her life? Would she have met and married Darren? Would she have had her two girls that she loved with every fiber of her being? Probably not.

Her father's words came back to her. *"Are you willing to disrupt your daughter's life to satisfy your own selfish desires?"*

Would it really be such a bad thing to reach out to the young woman? At this rate, it looked as if it was better to leave well alone.

Her mind flashed to the night before at Darren's office, and she cringed, mortified by her behavior. She couldn't understand why she had ended up there when they weren't even friends, and he wasn't aware of what was causing her predicament. The only consolation from the experience was that he hadn't realized that the daughter that she needed to find wasn't Emma when she'd let it slip that she needed to find her daughter. He'd tried his best to comfort her that Emma was fine as he'd spoken to her that day, and she had told him she was in Amsterdam. He'd allowed her to cry on his shoulder as he promised her that he would always be there for their daughters and that he wouldn't let anything happen to them. It became awkward after she disentangled herself from him. Not knowing how to process what had transpired, she'd simply thanked him and hightailed it out of his office.

The chiming of the bells by the door caused her to lift her head. "I'm sorry, but we're closed for the d—" Kerry stared in surprise at the man that had just walked through the door.

"Darn it! I was looking forward to having a cup of that

great dark roast and some butter tarts." Ethan smiled at Kerry, the dimple now more pronounced ever since she had discovered it.

"What are you doing here?" she asked, knitting her brows. "I'm sorry that was rude," she apologized, realizing that her words had come out sounding defensive.

"That's fine," Ethan replied, a smile still on his lips, his sharp gray eyes sparkling as he continued to look at her. Kerry felt self-conscious under his unwavering gaze and found herself fidgeting as she averted her own gaze. "I was in the neighborhood. I was doing a walk-through to compare the company's plan with the space they're planning to buy," he informed her, holding up what looked like blueprints.

"Oh," Kerry replied dryly, her mood souring even more than earlier.

Ethan continued to stare, but Kerry kept her eyes on everything but him. "Are you okay?" he finally asked.

"Never been better," Kerry replied in a high-pitched voice as she feigned a smile.

"Are you sure?" he asked, walking closer to the counter. "You look down."

Kerry blinked several times, surprised by his perceptiveness. "I'm fine," she stressed. Ethan remained silent, watching her. Kerry turned away from him. "I'll make you that cup of coffee, but there are no more butter tarts," she stated, filling the tension-filled silence with her words. "Those are made fresh like most of the other pastries here."

"Okay," Ethan replied, and she chanced, looking at him over her shoulder. Catching his gaze still on her, she quickly looked back around as she placed the ground beans in the machine and switched it on.

She heard him release a long breath which caused her to turn and face him out of curiosity.

"Look, Kerry. I get that you're put off by the impending sale

Fall is in the Air

of the other small businesses and the possibility of having to se—"

"That is the furthest thing from my mind," she interrupted him, tipping her head side to side as she closed her eyes for a brief moment.

"Penny for your thoughts?"

She opened her eyes to see him staring back at her, a small encouraging smile turning his lips up. It was her time to sigh. She rotated her shoulders to loosen up the tension there.

"I promise I'm a good listener, and I won't pass judgment," he continued to say when she hadn't immediately responded.

Kerry wasn't sure what it was about him, but she had a distinct feeling that she could trust him, and she felt the urge to divulge everything to him, but she rethought it and thought about sharing only some of her fears and concerns.

"Let me finish making your coffee first," she said.

"Fair enough," he returned and stood by the counter, watching her pour the liquid into the tall disposable cup before adding cream and sugar.

"Would you like a muffin?" she asked him. "I made them yesterday afternoon, but they're still fresh."

"Sure," Ethan accepted.

Kerry gave him the items. "They're on the house," she told him when he started to reach into his pocket. She followed him to the table furthest from the storefront and sat.

Ethan took a sip of the coffee and hummed in appreciation. "This is really good coffee," he complimented.

Kerry gave him an appreciative smile.

"So, what has you feeling down?" he asked after another sip of the dark beverage.

Kerry chuckled, shaking her head. "You really don't quit, do you?"

"I am as determined as they come," he replied with a mischievous smirk.

Kerry smiled back at the man, but it slowly turned into a frown. "I don't know where to start..." She sighed, and Ethan waited patiently for her to start. "I guess, sometimes I just feel like I wasted a good portion of my life making the wrong decisions. I feel as if I've allowed others to dictate what was best for me— my family, my husband, my children— and now I am having so many regrets, you know? It's like it is so deeply embedded in me to make the choices that will make everyone else comfortable that I've never really chosen myself, and now with the choices, I am choosing to make for myself, my sanity...my happiness, it's as if they're going to hurt so many people and make others uncomfortable and now I don't know if I have the strength to do it anymore." Kerry sighed, her shoulders sagging as she stared at the patterned tablecloth. "I just don't know where to go from here," she finished.

"These choices that you have to make, do you believe they're integral to your own growth and development?"

Kerry looked up at Ethan, whose steel-gray eyes stared at her in all seriousness. "I don't know...I guess."

"Kerry, listen to me," Ethan spoke, his commanding voice drawing her attention. "You need to do what's best for you, not anyone else. From what I have seen and come to know about you is that you are resilient. You're a fighter. You are someone who isn't easily swayed by the mammoth roadblocks."

Kerry stared wide-eyed at the man, surprised by his description of her.

"If the people that are in your life love you, they will respect your decisions even if they're not in total agreement with it. Whatever it is that you must do, do it and stop second-guessing yourself," he continued to encourage her.

"You don't know how much I needed to hear those words. Thank you," Kerry spoke with a grateful smile. Acting off her emotions, she reached over to rest her hand on top of the one he had resting on the table. "I really appreciate it."

Ethan gave her a warm smile as he flipped his hand over so that their palms were connected, and he intertwined their fingers. "I'm happy I could help. You deserve it," he replied.

Kerry's heart thumped wildly as she stared from him to their connected hands. She felt goose bumps rise along her arm and the back of her neck tingled. It shocked her that she could respond so easily and in such a way by just being connected to his hand. She returned his smile as she slowly moved her hand out of his.

"So, what else do you have planned for today?" she asked, changing the subject.

"Why, are you planning to come with or maybe go out on another nature trip?"

"No, not at all." She chuckled. "I was just curious how many more shops you're planning to stop at. After all, you are working for the interest of your client."

Ethan's gaze became guarded, a small frown forming on his lips. "You know this isn't a ploy to get you to sell, right?" he asked.

Kerry widened her eyes at the implication. "Of course, I know that. I didn't mean to...I'm sorry, I shouldn't have asked you that. Seems I just keep putting my foot in my mouth," she apologized. She slapped her hand against her forehead in trepidation.

"It's okay," Ethan replied, giving her a reassuring grin. "I do have to go now, though," he said, lifting the coffee and muffin into his hands.

"All right," Kerry replied, simply walking to the door with him.

"Ethan," she called out as he pushed open the door.

Ethan turned to look at her.

"Thank you," she said with much feeling. Ethan gave her a warm smile that caused her heart to skip a beat.

"You're welcome," he responded before pushing open the door further and leaving.

Kerry released another exaggerated sigh as she turned the lock and made her way to the kitchen. She needed to do something with herself, and at the moment, baking something seemed like the best solution. She spent the next few hours doing just that while trying to keep her mind off what had transpired between her and the man with the steel eyes. That was one area that she couldn't dare venture into. She was grateful for the advice he had given her, though, and it was that advice that found her looking up private investigators that dealt with special cases like hers.

Finally, she found what she hoped was the best man for the job. She got him on the second ring, and after explaining her plight, he agreed to take the case.

She hung up feeling satisfied, hopeful that she could find her long-lost daughter.

Chapter Thirteen

"I'm telling you, it was totally wild," Andrea cackled, holding her tummy as she threw her head back with mirth.

Kerry chuckled at her cousin's hilarious account of an incident that happened while she lived in New York. Andrea had explained that it was back when she was working two jobs to support herself and her three-year-old daughter, Rory, while also attending community college.

"I was killing roaches as quickly as my hands could bring my shoes down on their heads, and don't get me started on the rats...they were some monsters... like this..." Andrea drew back her arms to show the others the supposed size of the vermin.

Some of the ladies laughed while other people's eyes became as wide as saucers.

"I couldn't leave anything around the apartment unattended. I literally had metal safes to store my groceries."

"Oh my gosh, that's awful," Shelby, one of Andrea's friends, exclaimed, horrified.

"That's not even the worst of it," Andrea warned. "I came

in from work one day; Rory was still at preschool, so I thought to myself maybe I could take a shower before I went to pick her up. So, here I am in my towel, and I enter the bathroom, and I pull back the shower curtain to the shock of my life..." Andrea placed her hand over her chest and shook her head as if she was back at the scene experiencing it for the first time.

"What?" the others chorused, completely invested in the story.

Andrea turned and opened her eyes wide as she stared at each member at the table. "There was a rat in the bathtub, standing on two of its legs as it reached up to catch the drops from the dripping faucet and rubbing it over its fur," she whispered, cringing.

The others cringed as well, repulsed by the image she was painting for them.

"You should have reported your landlord to the Apartment Maintenance Complaints Department," Sharon, Kerry's sister-in-law who ran a law firm with her brother, spoke up. "They would have shut that place down quick."

"But then I would have been out of an apartment and living on the streets, Sharon," Andrea returned. "Have you seen the cost of living in the tri-state area? Even back then, the apartments and everything else was pretty pricey."

"I know it might have been hard on you, Drea, but it's unacceptable to live in such deplorable conditions when these so-called landlords charge you high prices and stuff you in a building that's not fit for...anyone," Sharon argued.

"I had my daughter to think about," Andrea deadpanned. "So, the decision to file a complaint, yeah, it did cross my mind but knowing where me and my daughter would be sleeping if they condemned the building made me put that thought on pause."

The table became silent as tensions rose. Gone was the

happy, free-spirited fun stimulated by the liquid courage that they were having.

Kerry stared at Cora, who stared back at her, communicating with her eyes that they needed to do something quick to ease the tension, or their girls' night out would end in disaster. Kerry knew Sharon could be a lot to handle as she was a methodical person who thought that everything could be solved using logic. They didn't always see eye to eye, but Kerry learned to somewhat agree with her and move on from the situation.

"But—"

"All right. Who's up for another round?" Kerry asked, clapping excitedly, drowning out whatever Sharon had been about to say.

"I'm in."

"Me too." Soon most of the table indicated that they wanted something from the bar.

Kerry signaled to the waitress who had just finished serving the booth two tables away from theirs.

The woman dressed in black jeans and a white top came over with a tray in her hand

"Hi. What can I get you?"

"I'll have a whiskey sour," Kerry ordered.

Cora followed suit. "I'll have a strawberry daiquiri."

Soon the whole table was ordering their drink of choice, quelling the previous conversation. Soon they were all laughing and reminiscing about their time back in high school.

"Well, I ran away with my boyfriend and ended up all the way in Texas," Kerry found herself giving away after the second drink she had been sipping forever. "Back then, I was into you if you were a leather-wearing, long-haired rock star. Only it didn't work out the way I had expected. The guy told me it was over, we were done, and all I had was the clothes I'd brought and about twenty bucks," she revealed, her voice becoming serious as the weight of her sharing got to her.

"I remember that." Tessa laughed. Her light brown hair that was framing her face bounced with the movement of her head. "Mom told us that Dad was leaving to get you because you'd gotten yourself in some difficulties. We thought Dad was coming to bail you out of jail, especially when Mom said you guys still hadn't made it back home after more than a month had passed. Ben and I even made a bet about that."

"Right, because I'm the screwup in the family, right?" Kerry chuckled, lifting the cocktail glass to her lips, and sucking up some of the martinis through the straw.

Tessa furrowed her brows, her blue eyes blinking rapidly as she tried to clear some of the fog from her brain. "I didn't mean t—"

"I mean, let's face it, I've always been the one that Mom and Dad have to be bailing out of scrapes. The one you all had to keep an eye on because I wasn't the perfect sister getting straight A's or the responsible brother who was also a star athlete. Nope, I was just poor old Kerry who can't seem to do anything right."

"Kerry, sweetie, I wasn't trying to offend you. I promise," Tessa tried to convince her sister, sobering up at the seriousness of the situation.

Kerry gave her a small smile that barely caused her lips to rise. "You might not have meant it, but it was implied. Perfect Tessa could have gone traipsing across states with her rock star boyfriend, gotten pregnant, and you wouldn't have to give the baby up because you could do no wrong in Dad's eyes."

"That's not true, Kerry. Why would you say something like that?" Tessa asked, clearly upset at her sister's words.

Kerry widened her eyes in surprise at the words that left her own mouth. "Forget that I said anything," she implored.

Tessa furrowed her brows once more. "No," she responded,

folding her hands and leaning back against the cushioned chair. "I need to know why you would use something like this," she repeated.

Kerry released a long breath. "It was just an illustration of how much your indiscretions wouldn't have moved Dad to action the same way it did for me," Kerry threw back at her sister.

"Honestly, Kerry, I understand where you're coming from."

Kerry and the rest of the group turned their attention to Andrea.

"That's how I felt for a long time. Like my decisions made me the worst of my siblings. I felt like the black sheep, especially after everything that happened with Rory's father." Andrea hung her head and played with her fingers as her hands rested on the tabletop.

"We've never thought of you that way, Drea," Cora spoke softly to her sister, reaching over to put her hand atop hers. Josephine did the same. Andrea raised her head to give them grateful smiles.

"I know that now," she responded. She then turned to Kerry as she said, "That's why I know that it's important that you talk about the issues you have but also that you can't allow it to define the bond that you get to have with them. Me, Cora, and Jo reconciled our differences, and we are better because of it. We support each other, and we try to be as honest with each other as much as we can, even if it might hurt. No relationship is easy, but if it's worth it. It's worth doing your best to preserve it."

Kerry nodded before reaching for her glass once more.

"I know how hard it can be, especially when you have different experiences with the world, but you and Tessa, you guys, I believe that you can get past the hurt and disappointment to become closer."

"You're right, Drea," Tessa responded before turning her

attention to Kerry. "I'm sorry for ever letting you feel like you were less than, Kare Bear. The truth is, I admire you."

Kerry stared at her sister in surprise and skepticism.

"It's true. I admire you, Kerry. I admire the fact that you've always been fearless, that you take risks and chart your own path. The fact that you were able to pick yourself up after your divorce to start your own business and how resilient you have been in fighting to keep it is inspiring. I am in awe of you."

Kerry placed her palm against her hot cheek as she stared at her sister in wonderment. She had never expected those words from Tessa. She wasn't even aware that she had been observing her so closely.

"You...you don't know how much hearing those words from you mean to me," she spoke with much feeling, placing her hand on her chest as her heart felt as if it would explode from the degree of warmness emanating there.

Tessa's lips upturned in an earnest smile.

"I'm sorry for what I said earlier. I shouldn't have, and the truth is that I admire you very much, Tess. You've always known what you wanted, and you worked hard toward getting it. I've never seen anyone work as hard as you, Tess, and it's what motivated me to do my best back when we were younger, but..."

"You also needed to chart your own path, decide what was best for you," Tessa finished for her.

"I love you, Sis," Kerry told her.

"And I love you. Very much." Tessa reached over to squeeze her hand lovingly.

"Great! Now that we've finished our one-on-one therapy session, let's return to the reason why we're here, ladies...to have fun." Kerry held her drink up in a cheer, and the others followed by their own glasses as they let out their own bellows of cheer.

A half hour later, Kerry, like most of the women at their

booth, was sporting a buzz. The conversations flowed freely, and their laughter rang out uncontrollably. When it was time for them to leave, the women packed up in the minivan, and Marg, who had volunteered to be the designated driver, got in the front seat, ready to drop them all off.

When she walked through the front door of her apartment, she made a beeline for the bedroom. She removed her bandeau dress and her high heels before reaching for an oversized T-shirt to put on. Kerry fell into the bed and allowed sleep to take over.

Chapter Fourteen

Kerry bopped her head to the upbeat song playing over the stereos as she kneaded the dough for the cinnamon buns she was planning to make for later. Anne went to buy well-needed supplies for the bakery, so she used the alone time to groove while she prepped, as Anne was normally bothered by anything that caused her heart to rise. She reached for the remote to lower the volume as she was certain she had heard the distinct musical chimes of the buzzer out front. Sure, enough, the sound rang through clearly the second the music wasn't loud enough to drown it out.

Kerry went over to the sink to wash off the caked-up flower and stickiness from her hands before rolling off a piece of paper towel to wipe them. She made her way toward the metal door and pushed it open, furrowing her brows as the shop wasn't due to open for another two hours. *Who could be at the door at this time?*

When she rounded the counter and made her way over to the door, her hands flew to her mouth in surprised joy at who stood behind the clear glass. She hurriedly unlocked the door and pulled it open.

"Oh, honey, I'm so happy that you're here," she spoke with much exuberance as she brought her daughter into her arms and hugged her tightly against her.

"Hi, Mom," Sophia responded against her mother's shoulder as she hugged her back.

When the two separated, Kerry held her daughter at arm's length, looking her over.

"What is it?" Sophia asked, self-consciously looking down at herself.

"Nothing, sweetie." Kerry smiled. "I just wanted to make sure that the school sent you back to me in the same condition you left in or even better."

"Haha. Funny, Mom," Sophia responded with a playful roll of her eyes.

"How are you here, though? We're in the middle of October. Isn't your break supposed to be a week away?"

"It should have," Sophia agreed. "But my last exam was two days ago, so I applied for early leave, and it was granted. So, here I am," she finished with a sweeping gesture.

"Okay, I got you." Kerry reached over to touch her daughter's honey-blond curls, running her fingers gently through them. "I'm glad you're here," she informed her, her lips turning up in contentment.

"I am too, Mom," Sophia replied with a smile of her own. "Something smells good. Were you making pastries?" she asked, looking behind her mother to the kitchen.

"I was," Kerry told her, her face shining brightly. "You're just in time to help me finish kneading the dough for two batches of cinnamon rolls."

"Oh, man. I should have gone to visit Dad first, then come back here to eat the finished buns." Her daughter pouted playfully.

Kerry lightly swatted her daughter. "Well, I'm glad you didn't."

Sophia followed her mother to the kitchen, and Kerry gave her an apron to put over her clothes after she'd washed up.

"Does your father know you're here?" Kerry asked as she worked side by side with her daughter, kneading and flattening and stretching out the dough.

"No, not yet. I was planning on surprising him like I did with you," her daughter said.

"All right." Kerry nodded. "Am I supposed to expect any more surprises from perhaps a certain long-missing daughter?" she asked.

Sophia laughed. "Mom, you know Emma is determined to finish out this gap year she took with her travels in Europe, so there is no way we're going to see her until that time," she reasoned.

"I know. It's just... I miss her so much sometimes." She sighed.

"Mom," Sophia spoke, drawing Kerry's attention. "Emma is fine," she reassured her.

Kerry rested her flour-dusted hands on the flat table, rolling her shoulders and dropping her head between the blades. She released a sigh. "You're right," she relented.

Sometimes she regretted giving Emma the option to go out of the country by herself for such a prolonged period of time, but if she had learned anything from her own father's heavy hand, it was that if she didn't give her space to make her own decisions, then she ran the risk of resenting her or worse— making choices that she would regret. Darren had been against it to the point that he blamed her for Emma's supposed "waywardness." It had always been that way with them where he thought that he knew what was best for the girls to the point that he had drowned out her suggestions. That was one of the reasons she couldn't remain married to him— he didn't value her input, and somewhere along the line, she had lost herself in doing exactly what he wanted and drowning out her own authentic self.

An hour later, the mother-daughter duo had pulled the cinnamon rolls out of the oven and placed the trays on the iron tabletop. The steam rising from them filled the air with the strong cinnamon scent.

"Mmm, these really smell like heaven." Kerry laughed at her daughter's expression as she bit into the soft, gooey roll. Slowly, Sophia opened her eyes with a sheepish look.

"I'm going to head over to see Dad. I'll see you at home in a few."

"Okay," Kerry replied. "I'll see you when you get there. We can finish our talk later." She reached over to give her daughter a kiss by her temple.

After Sophia left, Anne arrived with the ingredients she needed.

"I had to go to four different stores to find this quality," Anne informed Kerry, holding up the small bag of truffles.

"Anne, you are a godsend," Kerry complimented the woman, reaching for the bag. She held it to her nose and inhaled the deep musky aroma that had a hint of a chocolate scent as well.

"I really don't understand what could possibly be so great about a bunch of musty old fungus. It sure doesn't taste all that appealing to me," the woman replied, making a face.

"To each their own, Anne, to each their own," Kerry returned, placing the bag into her personal shopping bag. She planned on making black truffle pasta later, which she would be enjoying with her daughter now that she was here.

"Did you get the chocolate mousse?"

"Right here." Anne held up the tin of mousse.

"Great because we're completely out."

The two spent the next half hour setting up the display

cases and setting the espresso machine. Soon the customers started arriving, and by half day, they had to be preparing more baked goods for the customers that would be stopping by after work for to-go kits.

She stood by the service counter, wiping it down when the bells chimed. She looked across the room to see her cousin Andrea and her daughter Rory entering.

"Hey, you," she greeted with a wide grin. She came from behind the counter to greet the two women with a hug.

"Hi, Kerry," Andrea said.

"To what do I owe this visit? Wait, don't tell me," she said, eyes glinting with excitement. "You've decided to have the wedding in Oak Harbor."

Andrea and Rory smiled in confirmation.

"Oh great," she exclaimed excitedly. "This is going to be the biggest wedding in town. I can already envision it."

"Hold on, Kerry. It's Rory's day, remember? She gets to choose how she wants it." Andrea chuckled at her cousin's over-enthusiasm.

"Forgive me. It's just that I haven't planned a wedding in a while, and I'm just so excited," Kerry replied with an apologetic look.

"It's fine, Cousin Kerry, I understand," Rory replied.

"None of that now. Just call me Kerry," she advised the young woman.

Rory smiled and nodded in agreement.

"So, when is the big day, officially?"

"Well, officially, being as we're no longer going to have the wedding in San Fran anymore, so we moved the date up from next spring to December twenty-third," Rory responded.

"Wow, that's two months away," Kerry spoke in surprise.

Rory nodded her confirmation.

"That means we don't have a lot of time, so we have to get started right away. Have you commissioned a caterer yet?"

"Um..." Rory hesitated.

"They haven't," Andrea spoke up. "We were wondering if you would be able to help with the catering along with baking the cake," she continued in a hopeful tone.

Kerry pondered the request. She did have a lot to do during the Christmas season, but she supposed she could make it work if she didn't take on any more work prior to all that she had already committed to.

"Okay," she agreed, receiving cheers of gratitude from the women. "I have Anne to help me with cooking, but I will need to hire another line cook and possibly waitresses," she contemplated.

"Well, that's the thing..."

Kerry looked at her cousin curiously.

"Jo and Daniel have also signed on to assist with the catering, so it would be a collaborative effort among yourselves, and Daniel said he would ask the waitresses at Willberry Eats if they would be available to serve at the reception, so that would mean that we're all set where catering is concerned."

"Not bad. You've already got the ball rolling. That's good," Kerry said, nodding in approval. "So, Rory," she said, turning to the ginger-haired girl, "What type of cake are you thinking: two-tiered, three, highly decorative, or simple and elegant?"

"I really have no idea," Rory replied, looking lost.

"That's fine. We'll take it one step at a time," Kerry assured her. "I'll have some samples to show you by tomorrow, and then we can decide on the flavor."

"Thanks, Kerry. I appreciate it," the young woman replied, a relieved smile grazing her lips. Just then, her phone rang. Kerry noted that her eyes widened in surprise before she schooled her expression. "I'm sorry. I need to take this," she excused herself, going through the door and walking some distance from the bakery.

Andrea turned to Kerry after some time of looking at her daughter.

"Is everything okay?"

Andrea sighed. "I don't know. I feel like there's something she isn't telling me. A mother always knows, you know?"

Kerry gave a curt nod of understanding.

"But she keeps me locked out of some parts, and I feel like it's because I kept the secret about her father from her for so long. It feels like as close as we still are, something changed after we went through all of that."

Kerry placed a comforting hand on her cousin's arm. Andrea turned light blue eyes to her. "Sometimes we do what we have to do to protect those who we love even if they don't understand. In time she'll get it, and I know you guys will get back to where you were."

Andrea reached up with her free hand to squeeze the arm resting on her arm in gratitude.

"Thanks, Kerry. I appreciate it."

"Don't mention it," Kerry brushed it off. "I saw Julia the other day. She's getting so big," she observed.

"Oh yeah. I think she's due in late January or early February," Andrea informed her.

"That's great," Kerry replied. "You know I admire her courage to choose to have the baby, but not just that...the fact that she is choosing to keep that sweet baby despite the many other avenues she could have taken. I really do admire her." A smile of adoration graced her lips.

"She's strong, just like her mother," Andrea agreed.

Kerry shook her head again in agreement, but as she thought about her little cousin's choice compared to the one she had to make all those years ago elicited a feeling of melancholy within her.

Chapter Fifteen

Kerry woke to her cell phone vibrating at the edge of her night table. Reaching for it and sitting up in bed, she brought the device to her ear.

"Hello?" she answered, still a bit groggy. She looked over at the digital alarm clock to see that it was 6:45 am.

"Ms. Hamilton. Hi, it's Peter."

"Yes, hi Peter," Kerry rushed out, more alert than earlier. "Did you find something; anything?" she eagerly asked.

"Sorry for calling so early. I did. Quite a bit, actually," the man responded. "It wasn't easy to get the information. I can tell you that."

That's why I'm paying you the big bucks.

"What did you find out?" she asked.

"The baby you're looking for was adopted by a couple in Seattle."

"Do you have a name?" she rushed to ask.

"No, I don't. These things take a bit more time and a lot of patience," the man cautioned. "I'll call you as soon as I have something more concrete for you."

"Okay, thank you, Peter."

After the call disconnected, Kerry sat up with her back pressed against the headboard, and her comforter pooled around her waist. The information the private investigator had just supplied her with played over in her mind as if it was on a loop. Her baby had been adopted by a Seattle couple. What were the odds that her baby would have ended up living so close to her? It felt surreal knowing that her daughter possibly had been within reach all these years, and she didn't know it. A few tears trickled down her cheeks as she stared at the empty space in front of her. Kerry's thoughts continued to plague her about the fact she could have passed her child on numerous occasions and not even know it was her.

At seven thirty a.m., Kerry got up and made breakfast for herself and Sophia, who hadn't gotten in until late last night as her father had taken her out to eat. So much for the plans she'd made.

"Mmm, something smells really good in here." Sophia yawned and stretched as she made her way into the kitchen.

"Morning, sweetie. Did you sleep well?" Kerry asked as she cut up strawberries to place atop the waffles she made.

"Like a baby," came her daughter's response as she drizzled syrup over her breakfast. She smiled at her response.

"I take it you had a good time with your father last night then," she surmised.

"We did," Sophia confirmed. "We went to that nice little restaurant that we used to go to by the marina back when you and dad...you know...when you were still together," Sophia replied, ducking her head.

"I'm glad you enjoyed it and...that you got to do it with him," Kerry spoke, giving her a reassuring smile.

One thing she had been grateful for throughout the divorce process was that the girls had not been bothered by their separation, and she was glad that neither she nor Darren had ever encouraged them to take sides.

After the two enjoyed the breakfast Kerry had prepared, Sophia informed Kerry that she would be visiting the Willberry property to visit Aunt Becky and the sisters.

Kerry left the apartment an hour later. When she got in, Anne was already in the kitchen baking.

"You know, I feel like I should put a tracker on you to monitor your movements. Maybe then I would actually be able to beat you to the punch," she told Anne.

"Even if you did that, you still couldn't get here before me," the woman spoke confidently, eliciting a chuckle from Kerry.

"You must have superpowers then," she concluded.

Anne grinned. "Who knows," she said with an air of mysteriousness.

Kerry reached for her apron and put it on before heading to the sink to wash her hands. She opened the refrigerator to get the items she needed. She had removed the items before her: eggs, cream cheese, heavy cream, gram crackers, and all the other condiments needed to recreate her special cheesecake.

Two hours later, an exhausted Kerry went to sit out at the front with a cup of coffee. As she sat by the table furthest from the glass-paneled entrance, she took the time to savor the hot beverage, taking a bite into her cream cheese bagel. The texture and taste caused her to mewl with satisfaction. Just then, the buzzer alerted her that someone was at the door.

Kerry made her way to the front to find Ethan standing behind the closed door, a bright smile decorating his face. She pushed it open to greet him.

"Why is it that you always arrive earlier than my opening hours?" Kerry asked him as she stepped aside, granting him entrance to the bakery.

"I like catching you in your element before the crowd

comes in," Ethan confessed as he followed her up to the service counter.

"Should I make you a cup of coffee?" she asked as she rounded the counter, already reaching for the coffee beans.

"Yes, please," he confirmed.

Kerry set the receptacle under the machine to collect the hot liquid as the beans infused with the water as it percolated.

"And to eat?" she asked, turning to find him watching her. Her heart skipped a beat as she kept her gaze averted, waiting.

"Can I have one of those muffins?" he asked, pointing to the glass display.

"Okay, there are oatmeal and blueberry muffins," she informed him.

"I'll take a blueberry one, please," he chose.

After pouring the coffee, she removed one of the blueberry muffins and handed it to him.

"Thanks," Ethan responded. "Can you sit with me? I need to run something by you," he requested.

Kerry raised a brow in question. "Sure," she agreed, still sounding unsure of herself. She followed him to the table she'd previously occupied and took the seat he offered. Ethan sat across from her. "So, what do you need to discuss?" she asked. She watched him as he took a bite of his muffin. He chewed as he nodded appreciatively. Finally, he turned his silver-gray eyes on her trapping her in their depths.

"I wanted to update you that I am thinking about not pursuing this deal anymore," he confessed.

Kerry widened her eyes in surprise. "You're kidding right now, aren't you?" she asked warily.

"No, I'm not. However, I haven't come to a conclusion about this yet, but I have given a lot of thought to it."

Kerry smiled. "Knowing that you're reconsidering the sale is good enough news for me right now," she confessed.

Fall is in the Air

Ethan grinned. "That's partly the reason I came to see you," he informed her.

"Oh?"

"Well, my daughter is getting a break from her clinical rotations at Seattle Grace next week, so she's coming to visit me here for a few days at the inn. I was wondering if you could maybe...well, maybe you could show her around town for me," he requested.

Kerry smiled again. "It would be my pleasure."

"Thanks, Kerry. You don't know how relieved I am. I'll be in meetings for most of the days that she's here, and I don't want her to be just cooped up in the room with nothing to do but watching her father work."

"Believe me, it's no trouble at all," she assured him. "I like showing off what this little town has to offer. I'm sure your daughter will become just as enamored with this place as it seems you yourself are becoming."

"Oh, you have no idea," Ethan replied with a soft chuckle. "Um, do you..." He paused, scratching the back of his neck. His gaze darted away from her.

Kerry furrowed her brows in confusion. *Why is he so hesitant to say what he wants?*

Ethan took in a breath and released it, looking visibly more relaxed than earlier. "I was wondering if maybe you had time to take a walk with me."

Kerry widened her eyes in surprise.

Ethan rushed to clarify, "Just around the area. I want to understand the whole dynamic of this place."

"Ah," she replied, looking away from him. She wasn't sure why his rushing to explain that he just wanted to get a better feel of the area scattered with other small businesses like hers had caused her mood to deflate slightly, but it wasn't something she could dwell on. The man looking back at her was expecting her answer. "Sure, why not?" she returned with a tiny grin.

"Great," Ethan replied, pleased.

"Let me just tell Anne that I'll be out for a bit," she replied. Ethan gave a curt nod of approval.

Kerry pushed open the small door to the service area before pushing the metal door to enter the kitchen. Anne was sitting on a stool, going through a newspaper. She looked up when Kerry entered.

"You and Mr. Handsome finished talking already?" she asked with a smirk on her lips.

"How did you..." Kerry shook her head. "Don't worry about answering that. We are going for a walk to take a look at the other shops around the area. I just came in to ask if you can manage without me for a while?"

"Pfft... What am I eight?" Anne asked in mock offense. "You just go on your little date with that fine gentleman. Everything will be great until you get back."

"It's not a date, Anne," she refuted, folding her arms over her chest. "As I said, I'm just showing him around because it might help him with his decision to advise the company not to try for a buyout."

"Stay as long as you like. I don't mind," Anne assured her with a knowing smile and a glint in her eyes, choosing to ignore Kerry's rationale.

Kerry shook her head as she headed for the door. "I'll be back soon."

"Enjoy," Anne called out in a singsong manner.

"Ready to go?" Ethan asked when he spotted her.

"Sure," she responded, then allowed him to escort her outside.

The bright sun scattered its rays of intense light on the earth, causing Kerry to squint as her eyes adjusted to the sudden brightness. She raised her hand, using her palm as a visor to shield her face. She looked to her companion to see him staring at her in amusement.

Fall is in the Air

"What?" she asked, self-conscious.

"You look cute when you knit your brows together like that, especially with the little pout on your lips when you're frustrated," he gave by way of answer.

Kerry ducked her head, wishing her hair was long enough to hide her burning cheeks. "It's, um, the sun. I didn't expect it to be so bright out," she said, trying to steer the conversation into safer waters.

"I forgot that you spend most of the day on the inside."

Kerry risked looking over at him, but he was now looking down the path. She took a couple of seconds to take in his side profile. The most prominent feature was his sharp jawline. It was so chiseled, it looked as if it was cut from diamond.

"Shall we?" Ethan asked, his eyes catching her off guard. She turned her face, feeling guilty for being caught staring.

"Sure." She stopped to clear her throat, which felt like a frog was lodged there. "Let's go."

Kerry walked down the paved path with Ethan by her side. She pointed out the shops to him, introducing him to some of the shop owners who, for the most part, had been wary of him when they learned he was working for Major Corp.

Kerry took him to her friend Lydia's ice cream parlor further out toward the highway. Unlike her, Lydia's shop was outside the desired buyout area for Major Corp.

Ethan bought ice cream for the both of them, and after catching up with her friend, he and Kerry were on their way heading back to the bakery. "Glad you chose to take this walk with me?" he asked suddenly, surprising Kerry.

"I am," she replied after contemplating for a moment what she wanted to say. Ethan smirked, but he didn't say anything.

The two walked in comfortable silence, each throwing glances at each other when they thought the other person wasn't looking. When their eyes would accidentally meet, they smiled sheepishly and looked away.

Kerry enjoyed his company; she couldn't deny that. It was easy to talk to him, and he made her feel safe, but the feelings that she felt rising to the surface whenever she was around him or just thought of him made her cautious. She wasn't looking for a relationship. She was still finding herself. She didn't need the complication of love or worse, Ethan was only in Oak Harbor to close a deal for his clients, and then he would leave. There was no need to make what they currently shared more than what it already was.

Once he was done wrapping up his business, he would be moving on, and so she would keep her cards close to her chest. That was for the best, she tried to convince herself. The only thing she wasn't sure about was how much it was working.

Chapter Sixteen

One week later

Kerry hugged the jacket she wore close to her as the cold autumn air nipped at her. Her nose stung from the chilly air, and she was sure it was tinted red. It was almost the end of October which meant that winter was a short time away. Varying shades of yellow, orange, red, and brown leaves hung from the branches of their trees, with even more scattered across the earth, carried every which way by the wind unless raked and piled.

Kerry quickly made her way up the few stairs that led to the front porch of the inn. She would be meeting Ethan's daughter Ella today. He had called her yesterday to tell her that she was there, and he wanted to be a part of her first experience of the area.

Kerry had opted for a boat ride out to the Camano islands, then back to Fidalgo and Deception Pass.

When she made it to the lobby, Ethan was already waiting for her with a tall young woman with straight, golden hair that sat in a high ponytail. She was on her phone, her brows furrowed in concentration, so she hadn't noticed Kerry's approach. She took the time to look over the young woman. She had high cheekbones and a long, thin nose and her lips formed the perfect cupid's bow. She was a beautiful young woman, Kerry had to admit.

"Hey, thanks for coming on such short notice," Ethan greeted her, a wide grin on his lips.

Kerry matched his smile with one of her own.

"This is Ella," he introduced.

At the mention of her name, the young woman's gaze moved from her device to look over at Kerry. She was beautiful, Kerry thought to herself as the young woman whose deep-set eyes were a mixture of green and gold smiled at her.

"Hi, Kerry. It's nice to meet you. My father has told me a lot about you."

Kerry smiled, then shook the girl's hand. Her questioning eyes trained on the man behind his daughter. Her gaze flickered back to Ella as she responded, "All good things, I hope."

Ella laughed, the sound light and musical.

"If my father has nothing good to say about you, he won't talk about you. So, trust me, it's all been good," the girl responded.

Kerry found herself grinning from ear to ear as she raised a brow at Ethan, who stood by watching them carefully.

"Are you guys ready to go?" she asked, wanting to beat the morning sun even with the coldness she's experienced earlier.

"Yeah, let me just go and get the basket. You two can stay here until I get back," Ethan replied.

"So, your father said you're in your final year of med school?" Kerry turned to the young woman after Ethan went up the stairs to get the items.

"Ah, yes. This is my final year, but afterward, I have an

additional two years to complete my residency, and then I am all set," Ella responded.

"How old are you?" Kerry asked.

"I'm twenty-three. I started college just before my seventeenth birthday."

"That's um...wow," Kerry responded, impressed. "From what I can see, I bet you're at the top of your class." She found herself smiling at the young woman, already enjoying her presence even though they had just met. Kerry couldn't put her finger on it, but it felt as if she knew her somehow, even though this was their presumed first meeting.

Ella blushed. "Thank you. I do my best," she responded modestly.

"For what it's worth, just let me know when and I'll be your first paying patient."

"Thank you. I appreciate that," Ella replied with a broad grin on her lips.

Kerry looked above her to see Ethan by the landing staring down at them. She quirked a brow up at him, and he made his way down the flight of steps to join them.

Kerry led them down the cobbled path that led to the harbor and their mode of transportation for the day.

"This is the 'Silver Bullet,'" she introduced to them. The speed boat that was tethered to the dock swayed as the waves moved it back and forth. "My uncle named it after a movie that he watched with his daughters many years ago. It was a gift to his first daughter, Cora."

"That's a lovely story," Ella expressed.

"It is," Ethan agreed.

Kerry smiled sadly. "It is, but it's also filled with a lot of pain and regrets as well," she said. "But that story is for another time. We're out here to enjoy what the island has to offer, and as your tour guide, that is exactly what I aim to do."

After untying the boat, the trio made their way onto the

deck, and Kerry took the helm, steering it out into the deep. The motor revved as the watercraft sliced through the blue-green waters moving them further and further away from land.

"That's the Whidbey Naval Air Station." She pointed over to the rows of buildings and runways toward the east. There were a few naval air vessels scattered in the open spaces. Ella took out her phone and snapped a few photos. Kerry looked over at the girl and found herself smiling. It was as if she could feel the girl's aura, and she just knew that they would be in each other's life for a long time. She frowned, knowing that was impossible. Ella was going back to school soon, and her father would be returning to his life and his law firm. She turned her head to focus on the pristine waters before her. Soon her mind was taken over by the salty spray that brushed against her face.

"Are you okay?"

She turned to see Ethan looking at her carefully, his gray eyes probing.

"I'm fine," she replied, giving him a closed-mouth smile. "Just enjoying the scenery," she said, gesturing at the ocean. "We're almost at the Camano Islands. We can dock, and you and Ella can go get souvenirs from the shops if you'd like," she suggested.

"Okay, I'm sure Ella would like that," he agreed. "You're coming with us, right?"

"Of course. What kind of tour guide would I be?"

A few minutes later, they came into the alcove on the south side of the islands, where Ella got the chance to take photos of the beautiful mountain ranges in the distance before she brought them to the east so that the boat could be moored, and they could visit the island.

"Penny for your thoughts?"

Kerry looked over at Ethan and back at Ella, who was by the little food cart getting snacks. "I was just admiring how accomplished your daughter is. Her mother must be proud."

Fall is in the Air

A pained expression crossed Ethan's face.

"I'm sorry, did I say something wrong?" she asked, concerned.

"No, it's fine," Ethan assured her. "Her mother died ten years ago from acute myelogenous leukemia."

Kerry's hands flew to her mouth as her eyes widened. "Oh no. I'm so sorry, Ethan. I didn't know. I thought when you had mentioned that you were no longer in a relationship that it meant you were divorced. I am really sorry that you had to go through that. I can't imagine how hard it must have been," she spoke with so much emotion.

"It's all right," he promised her. "It's gotten easier with time, and plus, I had my daughter's well-being to think about. I couldn't just give up."

Kerry nodded in understanding.

"Your daughter truly is lucky to have you."

Ethan gave her a lopsided grin. "Speaking of which, I couldn't help but notice that there is an uncanny resemblance between you and Ella and that you both have so many similar traits. It's like looking at a younger and an older version of the same person," he mused.

Kerry chortled. "Are you sure you're not in need of glasses?" she asked playfully.

"I have a pair actually, only, I use them for reading and when I'm tired," he replied. "But seriously, I have been observing you both, and I can't shake the thought that..." Ethan's face scrunched up in concentration as he trailed off.

"That's just how it is sometimes, Ethan. You meet someone that you've never met in your entire life and have no relation to except for an uncanny resemblance to the other person. Usually, we call that God's weird sense of humor," she reasoned, bumping his shoulder with hers.

Ethan looked back at her and smiled but didn't say anything further.

After they'd eaten the corn dogs that Ella had ordered for them, they made their way back to the boat. Their next stop was Fidalgo Island, and then they went to the Deception Pass Bridge with Kerry giving them a brief history of how the magnificent edifice came to be. By late afternoon they were back at the inn.

"I had a great time, Ms. Hamilton-"

"None of that. Just call me Kerry," she encouraged the young woman.

"Kerry, I had a lovely time. Thank you."

"It was my pleasure, sweetie. I'm happy you enjoyed yourself."

After Ella went inside, she turned to Ethan.

"She likes you," he said simply.

"I like her too," Kerry returned.

"She doesn't normally warm up to anyone this quickly, especially after her mother...she really likes you," he stressed again.

"I'm glad," Kerry replied with an appreciative smile. "My family is having a barbecue next week. It would be great if you and Ella could make it," she invited, feeling hopeful.

"I will definitely be there," Ethan confirmed, smiling down at her. "I'm vouching for Ella that she will be there as well."

"Great, I'll let my family know. I'll see you later."

Kerry turned and began walking down the path.

"Kerry!"

She turned back to him.

"I had a great time too. Thank you."

A feeling of warmth bubbled in her chest, and she could feel her cheeks heating up as well. She gave him a short nod as a telling smile graced her lips. She turned and made her way to her car.

As she drove onto the highway, her phone rang. Kerry answered it over the car's Bluetooth. "Hello?"

Fall is in the Air

"Hi, Mom."

"Hi, sweetie," she chimed, feeling her day had just gotten better. "I'm so glad you called. How are you? How is Amsterdam?"

"Amsterdam was great, but now I'm in Cologne, Germany," her daughter told her.

"Wow, it's like if I blink too slow, you'll have visited all of the major cities by the time I open my eyes again."

"Very funny, Mom." Her daughter chuckled, and Kerry joined in.

"So seriously, how are you doing?"

"I'm great. My group met up with another group, and now we're planning to add a few more places to our travel map that weren't there before."

"Okay, honey. Please, just be careful, all right? Don't leave your belongings unattended, and don't take anything from anyone you don't know or trust."

"I know, Mom," Emma responded. "And I am being careful, like super careful."

"Okay, sweetie. I love you. I just don't know what I would do if anything ever happened to you, that's all."

"Mom...I'm fine. Relax. That's why we planned these weekly check-ins remember?"

Kerry bit her lip as she waited for the wave of apprehension to pass. "You're right, sweetie, and I am proud of you for being so responsible."

"Okay, thanks, Mom. I gotta go. We're going on a river cruise in a few, so I'll talk to you later."

"Okay, sweetie. I love you."

"Love you too, Mom. Bye."

Kerry sighed as the call disconnected. "Please let my baby come back to me in one piece," she whispered prayerfully.

Just as she made it to the apartment complex, her phone rang again.

"Hello?"

"Kerry, it's me."

"Darren? What is it?"

"I need you to come by the office," he spoke with urgency.

Kerry sighed. "I literally just pulled into my apartment. Can't this wait until tomorrow?"

"No, it can't," he replied.

Kerry perked up. "Why not? What's happening?"

"I think I found who the culprit is, and we have to act fast before they get wind of what's coming," he rushed out.

Kerry looked up at her building and exhaled.

"All right. I'm on my way."

Chapter Seventeen

"Hey, you made it." Kerry smiled broadly as she greeted the man who stood before her in a sky-blue polo shirt and long khaki pants. His dark-brown hair was swept back from his angular face, and he sported a bright smile as his gray eyes stared back at her.

"I did," he replied, cutting his gaze to look at the people milling around the huge backyard, chatting and laughing. "This is quite the soiree you all have going on here," he observed. "I like it."

Kerry felt a flutter in her stomach as Ethan spoke his approval while holding her gaze. Averting her eyes to look behind him, she asked, "Where's Ella?"

"She'll be here soon. She had an important call to take from school."

"Great," she replied, visibly relaxing at the news. She still couldn't put her finger on why she felt so close to the young woman, but the thought of her not being at the barbecue filled Kerry with a feeling she could only describe as disappointment which quickly dissipated with Ethan's words.

"Let me introduce you to the rest of the family and maybe get you something to drink," she offered after a few seconds of them just staring at each other, connected by some invisible thread that kept their gazes tethered.

"Lead the way," Ethan replied, holding his hand out before her in a sweeping motion.

"This is Cora, Andrea, and Josephine, my cousins. Guys, this is Ethan," she introduced him to the Hamilton sisters, who were the first ones they met as they made their way across the lawn toward the patio where most of the family was gathered.

"It's a pleasure to meet you," Ethan said, holding out his hand to greet them.

"It's nice to meet you too," Cora replied, giving Kerry a knowing smirk. Kerry, in turn, gave her a questioning look.

"So, you're the lawyer," Andrea spoke up with a confirmatory nod as if finally solving some top secret. A mischievous glint entered her blue eyes as she looked behind him at Kerry.

"Um, yes?" His answer came out sounding unsure as if he had just been asked a trick question.

Kerry narrowed her eyes at the sisters, silently commanding them to stop whatever it was they were doing.

"It's a pleasure to meet you, Ethan," Josephine jumped in, a wide, friendly smile on her lips. "We hope you enjoy the barbecue."

Kerry gave the youngest of the three sisters a grateful grin which Josephine returned.

"Yes, we hope you'll have a grand time. We're always happy for the additions to our growing family," Andrea chimed in, smiling knowingly.

"Thank you," Ethan replied, giving her a closed-mouth smile.

"Let me introduce you to the rest of the family," Kerry jumped in before anyone else could say something. "Excuse me, girls," she said, walking away from them, Ethan following her lead and excusing himself to fall in step with her.

She wasn't sure what her cousins were up to, but from their smirks and looks they kept casting on her and Ethan, she knew it was a matter of time before they took it a bit further, and she wasn't confident that their actions wouldn't embarrass her.

"Your cousins are lovely," he spoke beside her.

Kerry turned her head to look up at him. "They are," she replied fondly. "They can be a bit much as well," she added with a frown. "And that's typically everyone that is here," she realized with alarm. She prayed silently that none of her family members would do or say anything to make either of them uncomfortable.

She spotted Tessa sitting in a wicker chair with her daughter in the far corner of the patio. She guided Ethan in that direction.

"Hi, sweetie," Tessa greeted the moment she was in hearing range.

"Hi, Sis." Kerry leaned forward to accept the kiss Tessa placed against her cheek before turning to her niece and placing a kiss against her temple in greeting. "Hi, honey."

"Hi, Aunty Kerry." Dianne smiled up at her.

After stepping back, she turned to Ethan. "Ethan, this is my sister Tessa and her daughter Dianne. Ladies, this is Ethan."

"It's a pleasure to meet you both," he said, giving both their hands a tender shake.

After a few minutes of Ethan exchanging pleasantries with her sister, Kerry led him to meet some more of her family. She, however, steered clear of her father, who stood by the charcoal grill, flipping the burgers and hot dogs. She didn't trust that he wouldn't bring up the whole Major Corp deal if he found out that Ethan worked for them. She wasn't prepared for the back and forth with him in front of Ethan, especially since she was trying to convince him to get his clients to withdraw their offers.

She spotted her daughter coming from the main house with a casserole in her hands. When their eyes locked, Sophia's lips broke out in a wide smile. Her brown eyes left her mother's face to stare questioningly at Ethan beside her. Kerry walked toward Sophia with Ethan. The young woman placed the glass dish on the long stone table already stacked with other glass dishes, foil pans, and juice pitchers and made her way over to them.

"Sweetie, this is Ethan, the gentleman I told you about," Kerry spoke as soon as Sophia stood before them.

"Hi, it's a pleasure to meet you." Sophia smiled politely at him.

"It is a pleasure to meet you as well," Ethan returned, grinning broadly, "your mother has spoken highly of you."

Her smile widened even more, and she stared over at her mother with appreciation. "Mom said you have a daughter who is supposed to be here," she replied, her eyes searching for the young woman she'd never met before.

"Yes, she'll be here in a bit...wait, there she is."

Kerry and Sophia turned to see the young woman walking in their direction.

"Hi, I'm sorry I'm late," she apologized as she came to a stop at her father's side. Ethan wrapped an arm around her waist before planting a tender kiss against her temple. She, in turn, gave him a tender smile.

"That's fine. Your father explained everything." Kerry smiled reassuringly, her elation going up now that she was there.

Ella returned the smile, tucking in a strand of blond hair behind her ear.

"This is my daughter Sophia," Kerry introduced, moving aside so that the two could meet properly.

"Hi, it's a pleasure to meet you." Sophia stepped forward with her hand extended. Ethan released Ella, who extended her hand as well.

"It's nice to meet you too," Ella replied, her smile bright.

"Why don't I introduce you to the other young people that are here? They're more our speed," Sophia offered, looking over at her mother and Ethan, her expressive brown eyes conveying their meaning.

"Sure. Why not?" Ella agreed.

"Well, don't let us geriatrics slow you down," Kerry joked, holding her hands up.

"Thanks, old woman," her daughter replied with a smirk.

"Hey," Kerry harumphed as the others erupted in laughter. "You know I could have been your sister instead of your mother," she argued.

"You're right, Mom. You could be my sister...my much older sister. You're as young as you feel."

Ethan released an uncharacteristic snort which caused Kerry to turn and glare at him.

"Love you, Mom. No matter what, you'll always be my number one."

At her daughter's declaration, her lips upturned in a grateful smile.

The smile dropped when her daughter tacked on, "My number one old lady." Kerry gave her a deadpan look. Although Ethan managed to keep his laughter in check, she could see the slight shake of his shoulders as he turned his head, pretending to be looking at something across the field.

"Just go," she shooed her daughter, who now sported a wide grin at her expense, and Ella joined with a few chuckles herself.

Sophia and Ella turned in the direction of the harbor where most of the young adults had congregated.

Ella turned back with a conspiratorial look then she addressed her father. "Later, old man."

"Hey," Ethan called out, her words a playful jab toward him.

It was Kerry's time to chortle.

Ethan turned to her, a sour look on his face as the young woman walked away laughing.

"It's not funny," he whined, frowning like a child who just lost their favorite toy.

"Misery likes company," she returned with a satisfied smirk. At this, they both broke out in laughter. "I can't believe my own daughter called me an old woman. Now I feel like a frumpy old maid." She sighed.

"You're too beautiful to be an old maid," Ethan gave out.

She widened her eyes as she stared at him, dumbfounded. The butterflies in her stomach became a kaleidoscope. It felt as if everything was at a standstill for the two while everyone else carried on with the original timeline.

"What I meant was that you're too young to be an old maid," Ethan backpedaled, rubbing the back of his neck. "Not that you're not beautiful, because you are," he rattled on.

She gave him a small smile, not sure how to take his words, but then her smile turned to a frown when she noticed who was coming in their direction.

Ethan followed her gaze, visibly stiffening with the person's approach.

"Hi," Darren greeted the minute he was standing before her.

"Hi," she replied, casting her gaze on Ethan before looking back at him. "What are you doing here?"

"I needed to talk to you," he responded.

She exhaled inwardly. "And it couldn't have waited?"

"No." Darren looked at Ethan, then her, and back to Ethan, who stared back at him, grinning with a look of amusement.

"Darren, this is Ethan. He and his daughter are staying at

Fall is in the Air

the inn. Ethan, my ex-husband Darren," she made the introductions, trying to dispel the awkwardly tense moment.

"Hi." Ethan was the first to offer his acknowledgment, holding his hand out to Darren.

Her ex-husband looked down at the hand for a moment before he reached to shake it. "Hey," he responded before folding his lips in on themselves. "So how long are you visiting for?" he asked the minute their hands separated.

"Long enough to finish up some business, but who knows. I may choose to stay longer," Ethan replied, his own smile tight. His gray eyes glinted.

"Oh wait, aren't you that lawyer that's working with the company that's trying to get the small business owners to sell to build... what did they call it? The superstore of all stores?"

At the flash of something fierce in Ethan's eyes, a smile of satisfaction appeared on Darren's lips.

"You said you needed to speak to me. What is it?" Kerry interjected, the annoyance she felt coming out in her rushed tone and her brows drawn together as she narrowed her eyes to glare at him.

"It's a private matter," Darren replied, his gaze dancing between her and Ethan. "It's about the business."

"I'm sorry, Ethan, could you give me a few minutes to talk to Darren?" she asked, her tone much softer.

"Sure thing," he agreed with a smile that didn't touch his eyes. "I guess this is good a time as any to meet and greet more of your family."

She gave him an apologetic smile.

"Nice meeting you," he turned to politely say to Darren.

"You too," Darren returned, his lips turning up in a smirk as if he had just won the ultimate prize.

As soon as Ethan walked away, she turned to her ex-husband.

"Okay...what the heck was that?"

Chapter Eighteen

"What the heck was that, Darren?"

"What?" he asked, staring back at her innocently.

"You know what I'm asking. Why did you go investigator one oh one on Ethan like that?" Kerry folded her arms across her chest as she stared at him unblinking, waiting.

"I don't know what you're talking about," he replied, averting his gaze to look behind her.

"Oh yeah? How did you know that he was a lawyer working with Major Corp?" she asked, pointing out the obvious clues that gave him away.

His gaze darted around, never settling on her as he responded, "Sophia might have mentioned that you took him and his daughter on a boat ride."

Kerry rolled her eyes, annoyed. "So, you're using our daughter to spy on me now?"

"I wasn't spying on you," he replied, glancing around before looking back at her. "I was just curious. That's all."

"You can't do that, Darren. We're not together anymore.

We don't even get along. It's not your job to check up on my personal life, curious or not," she berated, throwing her hands in the air in exasperation.

"Shouldn't I be concerned when there's obviously something going on between you and the man that's working for the company threatening your business?" he asked pointedly. He folded his arms across his chest, his eyes challenging her to refute his claims.

"Who I'm involved with or what I do is not your concern. Not anymore," she stressed.

"So, you admit that you're dating this guy then?"

"First of all, this guy has a name, it's Ethan, and secondly, it's none of your business," Kerry simmered with disbelief that they were having this conversation. Her gaze darted toward the party. Apart from a few curious glances from her sister and a few from her cousins, everyone was busy conversing or eating to be concerned with what was happening between her and Darren. But then her gaze roamed until they landed on a pair of gray ones already trained on her. She quickly looked away.

"Look, I know we're not together, and we might not see eye to eye all the time, but I do still care about you, Kerry. You're the mother of my children, and I don't want to see you taken advantage of by a man who may or may not be using you to make his company's bottom line." Darren's gaze zeroed in on Ethan before they came back to her, imploring her to see his reason.

Realizing they were going nowhere in the conversation, she replied, "You don't have to worry about that because we're not dating. I was just being nice and showing him and his daughter that Oak Harbor is a great place... and, again, for the record, it's none of your business."

Darren's lips pursed, and he gave her a slight nod of acceptance. From experience, she knew he wouldn't let it go, and if she gave him another opening, they would be debating it again.

She would have to reset some boundaries after this thing at his company was put to bed.

"Why are you here again?" she asked.

"I don't think Irena pulled this off by herself. I think there is someone else on the inside that's involved," he explained.

"Why do you think so?" Kerry asked.

Her mind flashed back to the other night he'd called her to his office to reveal that the one siphoning money from their clients' portfolios wasn't his long-time business partner and best friend as they'd first thought but rather his secretary. After combing through the security logs, Darren had noticed a few anomalies that involved her, like the fact that she'd used her access badge on several occasions to enter his office after business hours. He was pretty sure he hadn't given her instructions to do so. He had been ready to confront her, but Kerry had managed to convince him to hold off until they'd gathered enough incriminating evidence to make sure she couldn't get away with it if she were indeed guilty.

"Chris, my IT guy said he went through the files on my computer, and he found a deeply embedded spyware. He called it a rootkit. It's installed to mimic my administrative privileges and duplicates the OS. He said that's why it was so difficult to detect. That's why we weren't able to trace the disappearing funds."

Kerry widened her eyes, and her mouth formed the perfect O, surprised by the level of malicious adware the person had managed to hide on his laptop.

Darren continued to speak. "Irena is proficient with computer applications, but for all intents and purposes, I doubt she is skilled enough to have embedded this file. So, either she's working with someone, or she's been a really good actor up to this point."

"What are you going to do?" Kerry asked.

He sighed. "Like you suggested... nothing. Chris is working

on tracing the phantom device, and hopefully, then we'll have our answer."

"That's a good idea," she agreed with a nod. "In the meantime, I'll come by the office to help you reorganize those files and complete the reconciliations as promised."

"Thanks," Darren replied with an appreciative smile.

Kerry gave him a closed-mouth smile. "And Darren..."

"Yes?"

"After this, stay out of my personal life. I mean it," she spoke, her tone full of warning.

Darren raised his hands in acquiescence. "All right, copy that."

This time Kerry's lips parted in a full smile. "Are you staying for the rest of the barbecue?" she asked. "You know you're always welcome. The parents still adore you."

Darren laughed at the nickname for Maria and Luke. It had first been used by their best man in his toast at their wedding, and it had just stuck.

"I'll be sure to greet them before I leave, but I can't stay. I have a few more loose ends that need tying up."

She inclined her head in understanding.

"Where's Sophia? I need to speak with her before I go too."

"She's down by the harbor," Kerry revealed, using her chin to point in the direction of the harbor.

After that, Darren left her to process her thoughts.

"Hey, are you okay?" Kerry glanced up from her musings to see Andrea less than a meter away from her. She plastered a smile on her face as Andrea came to a stop before her, handing her an iced tea.

"I am," she reassured her. Andrea nodded in agreement, but she stared back at Kerry with questions.

"We saw you were talking to Darren," Andrea said.

"He has a work issue that I'm helping him with," she replied, answering the unasked question.

"He came a long way to tell you something he could have otherwise shared over the phone," her cousin inquired with a slight rise and fall of her shoulders. "Are you sure he's not trying to rekindle the spark?" Her brows raised suggestively.

Kerry had to laugh at her antics. "Believe me, that ship sailed a long time ago. There is no way I'm boarding that again," she assured Andrea.

Her cousin's head bobbed up and down in acceptance. Kerry brought the glass to her lips and took a sip of the refreshing, sweet liquid.

"Lunch is served!"

The two turned their heads toward the patio where her father had made the announcement.

"Good, I'm starving," Andrea spoke, relieved as she started making her way toward the semi-closed area where they all would be enjoying the meal that was prepared for their get-together.

"You're always starving." Kerry laughed, moving off with her.

"That's because Mom watches the table like a hawk, making sure no one steals anything until everything's ready to be served. I stay away, making sure not to eat anything so that I can enjoy my meal better," Andrea responded.

"Oh, come on, Drea. You could have had a hot dog while you waited. Those were allowed," she reasoned.

"I know, but that's not what I want," Andrea replied with a shrug.

"Well, then you have no one to blame for your hunger but yourself."

Andrea turned to her cousin with a pout. "That's not true," she refuted.

Kerry gave her an "oh really" look.

"I present exhibit A," Andrea responded, gesturing to her mother, who stood at the buffet-style layout with tongs in hand. Aunt Becky looked up at her daughter with a suspicious glint.

"W...why are you pointing at me?" she asked, raising the tong to point back at Andrea.

"Nothing, Mom." Andrea smiled sweetly at her. "We were just talking about how sweet you are even though when it comes to the food at this barbecue, you're like a drill sergeant."

The smile that had made its way onto Becky's face slipped, only to be replaced by her glaring at her daughter.

"I still love you, Mom," Andrea rushed on to say in an attempt to placate her mother.

"That's the thing with children, Becky. They're always trying to rile up their parents." Maria, who stood beside Becky, chuckled at the exchange between the two before giving her own daughter a knowing look. "But we won't give them that benefit now, will we?"

Becky shook her head in agreement, giving her daughter a pointed look.

Kerry looked over at the small woman standing in front of her. She admired her strength. Her aunt was diagnosed with ALS, but despite her illness and with her daughters being back in Oak Harbor, it was evident that she was trying to maintain her best self, but they could all see that she was deteriorating very quickly.

"So, they're at it again, I see."

Kerry turned to her cousin with a knowing grin. "You know this isn't a barbecue if your sister and your mother don't have it out about the food."

Cora laughed at how true her statement was.

"What did I miss?"

"Brian, you're back," Kerry cheesed, rushing over to hug him.

"Hey, baby sis," the man greeted, hugging her tight against his chest.

"When did you get back?" she asked as they separated.

"I've been back since Wednesday," he replied.

"That's three days ago. Why didn't you call me?" she asked, swatting him across the chest.

"I told Mom, and Tessa and Charles know," her brother replied, rubbing the area of impact.

"Well, no one tells me anything," she replied, casting an accusatory glance over at her mother.

Maria paused, dishing out the mac-n-cheese to give her daughter a pointed look. "You would have known if you chose to check in more often."

She gave her mother a sheepish grin. "You're right. That's on me. Would you excuse me? I need to find my guest."

"Okay," they all agreed.

"Brian, I'm really happy you're back. We'll catch up later." She squeezed her brother's arm affectionately before heading in the direction where she saw Ethan chatting and laughing with Cora's and Andrea's love interests. She cringed inwardly when she noticed that her father was there too.

"Excuse me, gentlemen. I need to speak to Ethan," she expressed as she cut into whatever it was they had been discussing.

"Sure thing," they answered. Kerry smiled gratefully, careful to avoid her father's gaze that she could feel on her.

"I want to apologize for earlier with Darren. I didn't know he was coming," she told him as soon as they were out of earshot.

"That's fine. You don't have to apologize for something you had no control over," Ethan assured her with a charming grin.

"Still, you didn't deserve his hostility."

"It's fine," he reassured her once more. "I guess he felt threatened and thought he had to stake his claim."

"He has absolutely zero claim over me."

Fall is in the Air

Ethan turned his head to look at her as his lips curled into a smile. "That's good to know."

She whipped her head around to look at him, but he was already facing forward as they made their way toward the buffet-style table. He stopped abruptly, and she came to a halt beside him. She turned questioning eyes toward him.

"If I don't get a chance to tell you before this is over, I want to thank you for inviting me and Ella. I know she'll tell you herself, but this was great, and I'm happy that we could get to share this time together. It's been a while with her being away at school and me busy with work, but the time here on the island with you has made it very special." Ethan smiled down at her. His eyes shone with an emotion that caused a stirring in her chest.

"You're welcome," she responded, ducking her head to avoid his intense stare as her face warmed. "Let's go grab some food."

Chapter Nineteen

"Cheers to the weekend and cheers to another girls' night out, even if everyone couldn't make it." Kerry stood with her glass raised above her head.

"Cheers!"

The four other women sitting in the booth raised their own glasses in solidarity, cheering her on. She tipped back the small glass of bitter liquor. She flinched as it scorched a path past her tongue all the way to her stomach, setting it ablaze.

"I'll drink to that," Andrea said, standing and raising her own. She also tipped back the small glass, draining the content in one gulp.

Soon everyone was throwing back shots, the drink doing its job of loosening them up to have fun without consequence— at least not immediately. The only person not drinking was Josephine, as she'd volunteered herself to be the designated driver for the evening.

As the conversation flowed, so did the drinks.

"New topic of discussion," Andrea suggested, a mischievous grin splitting her face and baring her teeth.

Fall is in the Air

Kerry quirked a brow as she wondered what her cousin was up to. When she realized that Andrea's twinkling eyes were now focused on her, her heart dipped in her chest.

"Show of hands to those who were at the barbecue yesterday," Andrea told them.

Instantly, everyone raised a hand. Kerry raised her hand with the others, wondering where this little game was headed.

"Show of hands..." She paused to give Kerry a slow once over, smirking. "Show of hands to those who agree Kerry's date yesterday was handsome."

Just as quickly, the hands went up again. Only Kerry's hand remained on the tabletop, unmoving. Her heartbeat quickened, the crescendo causing a deafening roar against her eardrums and blocking everything else out.

Somehow, she managed to zero in on the fact that Andrea's mouth was moving again, and she tried her best to listen to her.

"Now, show of hands to those who noticed that he couldn't take his eyes off Kerry for most of the barbecue."

Again, all hands were raised, and each wore a wide grin.

"So, Kerry, what is the deal between you and Ethan?" Andrea directed at Kerry after her preamble.

Kerry sputtered, caught off guard.

"There is nothing going on between Ethan and me," she finally managed to say. "You're all making a mountain out of a molehill."

"Oh, come on, Kerry...anyone with eyes can tell that gentleman is captivated by you," Andrea interjected. "Even his daughter is captivated by you, who, by the way, bears a striking resemblance to you."

The nice buzz that the alcohol had given her was now almost completely gone as Andrea's questions and her sister's and cousins' curious stares filled her with angst.

"Guys, look, Ethan is a nice guy, but that doesn't negate the fact that he works for the company trying to buy me out." As she spoke, Darren's words played around in her head about Ethan only being interested in meeting the bottom line for Major Corp. Ever since he had said that, she found herself questioning how much of their time together had been used so he could come up with a plan to get her to sell Heavenly Treats.

"As soon as his business wraps up, he's out of here, so there's no sense barking up that tree. Plus, I'm not looking for a relationship. I just got out of one. I'm still trying to navigate this single-life thing. I'm not sure that's something I want right now."

"Kerry, you've been divorced for three years now. That has been a long enough time to find your bearings in this and figure out what you need." This time it was Cora that had said those words. "You can't close yourself off from finding someone because of what happened with Darren. Look at us. If we'd allowed in all the baggage from our past relationships, we wouldn't have found these wonderful gentlemen that made us believe in the beauty of love again."

Kerry looked over at Cora, then Andrea, and then Jo. Their eyes all showed their agreement with Cora's statement.

"They're right, Sis."

She looked down at the hand placed encouragingly over hers before turning to face Tessa.

"You deserve happiness. You need someone who matches your energy, and from what I've seen, Ethan does that. It's like you were destined to meet and be drawn to each other like this. I've seen the way he looks at you...It reminds me of how Don used to look at me." Tessa gave her a bittersweet smile as her eyes glazed over.

Kerry's heart warmed over from her sister's speech. It meant a lot to her that Tessa wanted her to be happy, and at the same time, it pained her to see her sister still hurting since the death of her husband two years ago. Theirs had been a match made in heaven that ended tragically. Tessa tried to be strong for her children and for the family, but Kerry knew that the pain was probably always close to the surface, and one word or memory about Don Luis was enough to cause tears. In that instant, she wished she could do something to take away the pain.

"Thanks, Sis," she spoke with fervor. Carefully she added, "I appreciate you, and I love you. I know you want this for me because I can feel it, but right now, I'm just happy that I have you as a sister and want to focus on strengthening our bond." She placed her free hand on top of the one Tessa had on her other arm and gave it a gentle squeeze.

"I'd like that." Tessa smiled, reaching up to brush across her cheek affectionately.

After their tender moment, Kerry turned to her cousins. "Thank you, guys, for always having my back." She smiled at them as well. That's how they had been as teenagers before everyone had gone off to chart their own paths, always looking out for each other. They had all been referred to as the Hamilton clan because they'd been so close back then. Her heart swelled with joy at the amount of progress that had been made over the past couple of months to heal.

"That's what we're here for, Kare Bear," Andrea replied with a grin. "To lift you up when you're down, to cheer you on when you're feeling your best." She paused to smile conspiratorially. "To talk about boys, like back when we were in high school," she whispered mischievously.

Kerry laughed at the others joining in.

Her mind flashed to the handsome gentleman, as the ladies had put it. In this instance of them voicing their opinions about Ethan and encouraging her to give him a chance, she couldn't hide from the emotions that had been brewing since the moment she'd met him. It was more than just his features that drew her to him. It was his easy nature, his obvious love for the outdoors, and how easy it was to talk to him. She especially liked how fiercely he loved his daughter. Those were all traits she wanted in a man if she was ready to date. But the thing was, as much as he checked almost all the boxes on the list, he would be leaving soon, and she wasn't looking to get into any romantic entanglement. Allowing her feelings to blossom any more than they already had was dangerous. So, she decided to table them. That meant she would have to limit their interactions as well.

That night as she lay in her bed, her thoughts kept replaying all that Andrea and the others had said. As much as she wanted to put Ethan out of her mind, he occupied her thoughts up until she fell asleep.

Her phone vibrating woke Kerry from her sleep the next morning. Reaching over to the bedside table, her hand moved over the surface until it made contact with the device as it vibrated under her palm. Eyes still closed, she brought it to her ear, not looking at the caller ID.

"Hello?"

"Kerry? I didn't wake you, did I?" came the deep masculine voice through the speaker.

"Ethan?" she questioned. Her heart drummed wildly as she struggled to sit up.

"Hi," he replied.

"Hi," she all but whispered as her breath snagged in her throat.

As a moment of silence passed between them, Kerry's mind had gone into overdrive, conjuring up the different reasons he had called her, but none of them prepared her for what he said.

"Can I invite you out on a jog with me?"

Her heart started to beat even faster.

"Um..."

"I'm asking because I still don't know the area, and you mentioned that you normally go on a run before the sun comes up. I was hoping you'd be able to be my partner today."

Kerry didn't know how to respond. Spending more time with Ethan wasn't wise, but she also didn't want to come off as distant all of a sudden.

"I would ask Ella, but she had a long night. Even though she's on break, she has so many assignments and deadlines. Plus, there's something that I wanted to talk to you about."

She held the phone tightly against her ear as she considered his offer.

"You still haven't said anything," Ethan reminded her after a beat.

"Where do you want to meet?" she found herself asking.

"Why don't you tell me where to meet you? You're the expert on everything that has to do with this town. That's what I'm relying on. I trust your judgment."

She couldn't help the smile that graced her lips or the warmth that bubbled in her chest at his disclosure.

"Okay, meet me by Windjammer Park, say in the next twenty minutes."

"All right," he agreed.

After giving him instructions on where to find the park, she swung her legs over the edge of her bed and walked to her bathroom to get ready. She willed herself not to examine her decision to go with him too closely.

Fifteen minutes later, she was at the park with five minutes to spare. It was enough time to lean against her car as she tried to decide if she had made the right decision to meet him. She wasn't hiding from the fact that she liked Ethan, but it wasn't something she was planning to act on, and she'd already concluded that it meant avoiding him.

The moment she saw the platinum SUV coming toward her, she straightened up. Ethan parked the car beside her before stepping out to come and join her. He was wearing gray sweat bottoms and a white T-shirt that stretched across his broad shoulders and firm pectorals as it showed off his lean physique. At his approach, her heart fluttered in anticipation.

"Hi," he greeted with a broad grin.

"Hi," she managed to respond against the protest of her throat that felt like a bag of sawdust.

"Ready to go?

Kerry nodded, not trusting herself to be able to speak again.

She turned toward the beach, and Ethan fell in step with her.

"We can start here," she turned to say. "The path goes on for about three miles, but we'll just pace ourselves and then come back here."

"Okay," Ethan agreed. "Lead the way."

She quickly turned to the path and took off. He maintained stride with her. Each time Kerry quickened her pace, he was right there with her until they were outright barreling their way down the sandy path.

When it felt as if her lungs would give out, Kerry came to a stop and gulped in bouts of fresh air. She looked over to see Ethan doing the same. His head turned to look over at her. The two stared at each other for some time until they broke out in laughter.

"I was beginning to think I did something wrong."

"Why would you think that?" Kerry asked the man as he came to stand before her.

"This morning, when I called you, you seemed ready to reject the offer to join me, and it felt like you were preparing to cut me off for good."

"I'm sorry about that," she apologized, straightening. "I admit I was feeling a bit hesitant because...well, your business here is almost coming to an end, even if there is no way in heaven I'll sell my bakery."

Ethan chuckled.

"I guess I was giving you an out for when you give me the

disappointing news that you've gotten the signatures of nearly all the businesses on my strip that have chosen to sell to your company."

"That's what I wanted to talk about after our run, actually."

She widened her eyes in surprise.

"I wanted you to be the first to know that Major Corp will be looking elsewhere to establish their business. Somewhere that will be completely outside of Oak Harbor."

"Oh my God. You actually did it," Kerry exclaimed. Without thought, her arms went around his neck as she was overcome with joy.

Chapter Twenty

Kerry knew that she needed to remove her hands from around his neck and step out of the embrace, but the moment Ethan brought his hands around her back to bring her closer, her resolve crumbled. She shivered involuntarily as his heady scent teased her nostrils. The woody scent of his aftershave combined with his own male musk made her want to lean even further into him, to press her nose against his neck, and become intoxicated with the very essence of him. But it was unwise.

Her hands loosened around his neck, and Ethan sensing her withdrawal, released her, stepping back. Kerry ran her right hand up and down her left arm nervously. She kept her gaze averted as she tried to bring her emotions back in check.

After a long period of silence, she spoke. "Thank you, I know this wasn't an easy decision for you." She lifted her eyes to look into his gray pools. "I appreciate you helping us to keep our businesses."

Ethan's gray eyes crinkled at the corners, and the impres-

Fall is in the Air

sion on his cheek deepened as he smiled broadly at her. "You're welcome."

Kerry's heart skipped a beat as her lips upturned in a smile all on their own.

"Do you have plans for the Halloween weekend?"

She was taken by surprise at the question but answered nonetheless. "Apart from a few pastry orders, no. I'll be at home with a bowl of candy by my door waiting for the trick or treaters to show up." Instead of asking the obvious, she gave him a questioning look.

Ethan scratched the back of his neck before clearing his throat. "I haven't done this in a long time," he said with a small laugh, averting his eyes and further confusing Kerry. Ethan released a long breath and swooped his gaze back to her. "There's a Halloween party being held at The Anchor. I was wondering if you would like to go...with me."

Kerry inhaled sharply as she widened her eyes with surprise. Before she could respond, he spoke again.

"I like you, Kerry. I have since the first day I met you," he confessed, staring straight into her eyes. "I wasn't planning on acting on it because I thought nothing would come of it, especially as we were on opposite sides of this acquisition, but the more time I spent with you and your family, the more I have come to realize that it's futile to deny my feelings for you."

Kerry's heart repeatedly slammed against her ribcage, her breathing coming out in rapid, audible breaths that lifted and dropped her chest in quick succession. She tightened her hand around her arm; her nails biting into her skin were sure to leave small crescent markings on her flesh. She couldn't think. She couldn't speak. All thoughts flew out of her mind except the words he'd just spoken.

"The time you spent with my daughter and how much she has come to adore you..." He stopped to release a throaty chuckle.

"She talks about you all the time. I marvel at how quickly she was drawn to you and how at ease she was in your presence. It's never been like that with anyone. That made me want to be a part of your world and have you be a part of mine even more. I like you, Kerry."

She still hadn't said a word. She couldn't formulate a coherent sentence. Everything was jumbled in her head. She opened her mouth to try to force the words out, but each time it felt as if a fist was secured around her voice box, blocking words from escaping.

"Please...say something," Ethan pleaded after more than a minute of her just staring at him in silence. "If you don't feel the same way as I do for you, that's okay," he continued to say when she still hadn't spoken. "I didn't mean to put you on the spot like that. I just tho—"

"I do," Kerry blurted. Ethan's eyes widened before they almost shuttered.

"I mean, I do like you," she clarified. At her confession, his silver eyes brightened, and he took a step toward her.

"But..."

Ethan stopped and looked at her cautiously.

"I don't think this will work. You're moving back to the city, and I don't see myself living anywhere else other than Oak Harbor. This won't work," she voiced, her eyes filled with the apprehension she was feeling.

At this, Ethan released another chuckle that confused her as he came to stand before her. "It's a good thing I'm not planning to go back to Seattle then."

Kerry stared up at the man looking down at her with a triumphant grin on his lips. "I reassigned my workload to be able to spend a few months here," he revealed.

"Why would you do that?" she asked him, alarmed.

Ethan stared at her for some time before he responded. "I'm not staying because of you, Kerry...well, technically, it is because of you, but I always want to learn about this place. It has intrigued me since the moment I took the case. I've been thinking about moving from Seattle for some time now to somewhere less busy, and this place is honestly a slice of heaven. After spending time doing all these things with you, it has become clear that I want to explore it more...with you."

If Kerry's smile could have broadened any more than it already had, it would have rivaled that of a Cheshire cat. His heartfelt words were enough for her to renege on her pact with herself after her divorce from Darren three years ago to never get involved in another relationship. She'd only tried the relationship thing twice, and both times had ended bitterly. She had planned to live her best life as a single woman who knew what she wanted and didn't have to answer to anyone or put a lid on her desires to please anyone. But at that moment, what she wanted was Ethan.

"Ethan, I—"

The ringing phone in the small pouch attached to her side stopped her from finishing her sentence. "I'm sorry, let me just put this on silent," she said, taking the phone from the pouch to turn off the ringer. She noted the number calling and turned apologetic eyes to Ethan. "I have to take this," she said.

"Okay."

Kerry lifted the phone to her ear, pressing the answer button.

"Hello?"

"Miss Hamilton, I have good news. I found your daughter."

"You have. Oh my God, John! This is...this...wow. Who is she? Where is she?" she rushed out.

"She was adopted by a couple that lives in Seattle. I told you that already. Her father is a lawyer, but her mother died quite a few years back when the girl was young."

Her heartbeat picked up momentum with each piece of information the PI revealed.

"Are you okay?" Ethan asked from beside her.

Kerry didn't look back at him, but she nodded that she was fine. She refocused on the call. She was almost afraid to ask the next question. She dreaded the answer being one that she already knew but still, she needed to hear the man say it.

"Wh-wha.." she swallowed against the lump in her throat. "What is her name?"

"Ella Sharpe. She's a med student at Seattle Grace."

The phone almost slipped out of her hand at the PI's revelation. She swallowed convulsively to wet her now parched throat, but it became difficult to do so as her muscle memory started to fail.

"Are you...are you...sure?" Her voice sounded distant, as if it was coming from across a valley rather than from her own lips.

"Kerry," she heard Ethan's concerned voice, but she couldn't focus on it. There was a ringing in her ear, and her breath felt as if it wasn't being sucked out of her body by an unseen entity.

"I'm sure Miss Hamilton," the PI affirmed before reading from what sounded like a list. "Ella Sharpe, medical student at Seattle Grace, adopted parents, Dana and Ethan Sharpe. Mother deceased."

The ringing got louder, and bile pooled at the back of her throat.

"Kerry...Kerry."

Someone was calling out to her, but she couldn't see them, not even when they took her face between their palms, forcing her to look at them or when they assured her everything would be fine.

"Kerry, stay with me," came the voice piercing through the haze, but she still couldn't respond. Her body felt weightless, and darkness took over her mind.

* * *

She was in the tulip field again. The colors were just as vivid as before. Kerry ran her hands over the soft velvety undersides of the flowers, relishing the sweet aroma that wafted up to her nose. She bent to inhale more of the fresh scent.

"Why are you here again?"

Kerry straightened up to see the same female standing a few feet away from her with her arms folded over her chest. She still couldn't see the young woman's face, but it was more defined than it had been the last time she saw her.

"I came to see you," Kerry replied, holding her hand out to her. "I came because I wanted to apologize for abandoning you and because...I know who you are."

"Bravo!" the young woman clapped loudly. "You finally figured it out. How delightful," she spoke, her tone scornful.

"Tell me, Mother, how does it feel to know that I have always been this close but somehow still out of reach to you?" she asked, walking toward Kerry. With every approaching step, her features became clearer until Ella was standing just a few inches away from her.

"Ella, please...let me make it up to you. I didn't mean to—"

"Don't make excuses, Mother. It's time to face responsibility for what you did. You abandoned me! There is no way I will ever forgive you for that, no matter what your reasons are."

Kerry jumped up with a start.

"There you are. Can you hear me?"

She blinked a couple of times until the concerned face hovering above her came into focus.

"Kerry, can you hear me?" Ethan repeated.

"What happened," she asked, propping herself up on her elbows. She noticed that she was in the reclined front seat of his SUV. She put her hand against her temple, feeling it throbbing.

"You fainted," he explained.

She furrowed her brows. "I did?"

"Yes, you did," Ethan repeated slowly. "One minute you were on the phone talking to someone named John, and the next you looked like someone had scared you to death, and then...you passed out."

It all came back to her in a rush. Her conversation with John, his revelation that Ella was her daughter, and then everything had gone black. Ella was her daughter. Her heart constricted at the knowledge. A myriad of emotions washed over her— relief, happiness, sadness, and terror.

"You're crying." Ethan reached over to tenderly wipe at the tears flowing down her cheeks. "What's wrong?" he asked soothingly.

Kerry's gaze turned to Ethan, glistening with the remainder of her unshed tears with guilt. This was the man that had grown her daughter as his own. The man who was responsible for the beautiful young woman she'd had the privilege of meeting last week. It had been one of the best days she'd had in a while. She remembered how close she had felt to her, how much she wanted to learn about her— about all her dreams and aspirations. Little had she known that it was her maternal instinct that had drawn her to her.

"Ethan, I need to ask you something...something very important," she said, her voice quivering as she stared at the man still looking at her with concern in his eyes.

"Ella...is she...are you..." She released a heavy breath before trying again. "Was Ella adopted?"

Chapter Twenty-One

"Is Ella your biological daughter?"

Ethan recoiled from Kerry as if she had burnt him. "Why would you ask me that?" he asked defensively.

"Ethan, please," she pleaded.

"First, tell me why you are asking me this?" he countered, his voice straining with frustration.

Kerry released her pent-up breath. Her throat felt tight, and her eyes blurred with tears.

"Look, Kerry. I need you to tell me what is going on...please."

"I had a baby when I was eighteen. A baby girl that I gave her up for adoption," she rushed out, turning her head straight to look through the windshield.

She heard Ethan exhale before he moved away from the door. Soon he was seated in the driver's seat opposite her.

"What happened?" he asked, his voice soft and encouraging.

"I was seventeen and in love..." She paused as she prepared to dredge up the past and the hurt that she'd left buried for so long. She felt warmth on her hand and looked down to see Ethan resting his palm on top in encouragement. She looked over to see him already staring at her, his eyes full of empathy.

Kerry turned her head back to the windshield and started again. "I ran away with my boyfriend and his rock band. We went everywhere and did everything together. I was his biggest cheerleader, and there was never a thought that we wouldn't last, so...I gave him everything." She sighed sadly, wishing that she'd held back, regretting how much shame she felt whenever she thought about Mark now.

"He started acting different, hanging around the wrong crowd, taking the phone numbers from his groupies, entertaining their arguments. I guess I was upset about it all, and I kept confronting him about it, and he kept apologizing and promising that he would do better. The funny thing is I didn't believe him, and I knew he would do it again, but I stayed. Then one day, he comes into the RV and tells me it's not working out, that I should go home. That it was over. I left that day, but I didn't go home. I was too ashamed to face my parents, especially my father. I didn't want to see the disappointment on his face or the I-told-you-so look, especially after I found out I was pregnant." Kerry paused as the weight of reliving all that had happened to her washed her with sadness.

Ethan squeezed her hand to remind her of his presence there, supporting her. She turned to give him a grateful smile.

"I didn't call my dad until I was over seven months pregnant because I was struggling, and I didn't know what to do. He came, and when he saw my belly, he told me I had a decision to make, become a mother when I clearly wasn't ready to become one or give my baby to a family that would be able to care for her. I wanted to keep my baby, but I felt like I had disappointed my father so much and that I had already ruined so many lives that I didn't want to ruin my little girl's life, so I chose to give her up for adoption." She broke down in tears, the

Fall is in the Air

sobs racking her body as she thought about her daughter, whom she had wanted so much but had given up because of the fear she felt. If she was able to have a do-over, she knew she would have chosen to keep her no matter what the struggles she would have faced as a single mother. She wept for the time that had been robbed from her in being a mother to her daughter.

"Hey, it's okay—"

"It's not," Kerry responded, turning her tear-filled eyes to look at the man staring back at her sympathetically.

"I gave away my child because I was scared. I was a selfish coward," she berated herself.

"You are not a coward, and you certainly aren't selfish," Ethan spoke up forcefully. "The woman I see before me is strong and brave. You did what you had to do to ensure that your child would be taken care of even if it wasn't by you. I would say that is the admirable trait of a good mother who would do anything to protect their child."

Her heart swelled with his words, and warm tears rolled down her cheeks. Ethan reached over to wipe a few drops away.

"You are strong, Kerry, and no matter what anyone else says or thinks, you did what you thought was right, and no one should hold it against you. If anything, you should let your father know how his actions have affected you, and hopefully, you can reconcile the past and move forward."

It was his turn to look away from her. The two stared out the windshield for a long time. The sun had risen high in the sky, brightening their surroundings and the car's interior with its rays of light.

"Maybe we can continue this back at your place or somewhere you'd be comfortable going to," he suggested.

"We can go to my place," she informed him. "Let me get my keys, and we can go."

"Are you sure you can drive?" Ethan questioned, the concern evident in his tone.

Kerry turned to give him a reassuring smile. "I'm fine, I promise."

He allowed her to go, and soon the two cars pulled away from the park and headed toward NE 10th Ave. before turning onto N. Oak Harbor Street. Fifteen minutes later, they were taking the elevator up to Kerry's apartment.

Kerry opened her door, allowing him access. "It isn't much, just a two-bedroom space. After my divorce, I decided to sell the house and move into something that's okay for me and when my daughters visit," she rambled as she led him from the short hallway into the open space living, dining, and kitchen area.

"It's nice. It looks very comfortable," he assured her with a smile.

Kerry ducked her head, suddenly feeling a bout of shyness in having him in her home, in her space.

"Would you like a cup of coffee or tea?"

"I'll have whatever you're having," he answered, his smile this time revealing his white, even teeth and the dimple that caused her to catch her breath. After offering him a seat on the leather couch, she busied herself in the kitchen. After setting the coffee machine to percolate, she removed what she needed from her cupboards to make waffles and went about mixing the ingredients for the next five minutes. Fifteen minutes later, she brought a cup of coffee and waffles with fruit and a topping of whip cream over to Ethan, for which he thanked her.

She sat in the armchair adjacent to him, and the two spent the next couple of minutes eating what she'd prepared. Kerry took his empty plate and cup to the sink.

"I can help with that," he offered up.

"You're a guest," she threw over her shoulders. "Plus, I needed to thank you for the Major Corp situation among...

other things." Ethan remained seated as he watched her at work. She could feel his gaze on her, but she schooled herself not to glance in his direction. When she was finished, she went and reclaimed her seat in the armchair.

After a few more minutes of silence, Ethan spoke. "My wife, Dana, and I, we got married pretty young. We were so in love and didn't want to wait to start our family. She suffered a miscarriage at twenty-two, and it was very devastating to both of us, but more so her. We then found out that she had womb cancer, and the only way to save her was to remove her uterus. She became very depressed, and no matter how I expressed that I would love her no matter what and that even if we didn't have children, we would be okay because I loved her for who she was and not what she was able to give me. But... it just...it wasn't enough for her." Ethan looked over at Kerry, his expression full of pain.

She found herself rising from her seat to station herself beside him. Automatically, she reached for his hand and entwined her fingers with his, offering him the support he'd given her earlier at the park. Ethan gave her a half smile.

"Two years later, she was still depressed. I had suggested adopting before, but she had shot down the idea because she wanted the baby to be a symbol of our union, our love, but that was impossible. So, after much convincing, she agreed. She was still hesitant and afraid that she wouldn't be able to love the baby like it were her own, but that all changed when we held Ella for the first time. I could see in her eyes that she'd finally gotten all that she desired."

Ethan looked over at Kerry, his eyes filled with the bittersweet memories of the past.

"No one loved that little girl more than Dana. She doted on her and made sure that she felt that she was loved at all times. We had a happy marriage, a happy family. We were happy."

Ethan whispered the last statement and then released a deep sigh.

"Thirteen years later, after having to remove her womb, she went in for a routine checkup, and she was informed that cancer had come back but more aggressively. Acute myelogenous leukemia. She fought it for a year, but it proved too much for her body. Chemo stopped working, the medication, everything. We spent the little time we had left with her at home, making sure she was comfortable and surrounded by those who loved her. She died telling Ella that she was the best thing that happened to both of us."

Kerry's free hand flew to her mouth, touched by the pain he had suffered.

"I'm so sorry you had to go through that," she spoke softly, wishing there was more that she could offer than just her words.

Ethan gave her a grateful smile. "After that, my only priority was Ella and making sure that she would have everything she ever needed in case anything happened to me. I threw myself into my work and taking care of her, and pretty soon, I was made partner at my firm. I would do anything for my daughter, Kerry." He turned to look at her, the magnitude of his words reflected in the serious glint in his eyes.

Kerry understood that look all too well. There was nothing that she wouldn't do for Sophia and Emma. They were like her lifeline, and now Ella had been added to that. Even though they'd only interacted a few times, there had been a strong connection there and knowing now without any doubt that she was her daughter, she felt the same level of protectiveness for her as Ethan did.

"I want you to know that I would never wish the pain and regret you've endured for the past twenty-three years, but I am also glad that they brought me my daughter. I have cherished that decision since the day I held her in my arms. I also know

Fall is in the Air

that it's going to be a hard task to get her to understand your reasons behind why you did what you did, but I'm willing to make arrangements for that if you are prepared to fight for her."

Kerry gave him a grateful smile, thankful that he had confirmed that Ella was indeed adopted.

"Does she know...that she's adopted, I mean?"

Ethan turned to look at her. "Dana and I chose to tell her the moment she understood what the words meant. We didn't want it coming out any other way or for her to hear it from anyone else," he confirmed.

Kerry shook her head in understanding.

"And has she ever asked about her biological parents—about me?"

Ethan gave her an apologetic look.

"No."

Kerry stewed in her thoughts, knowing that there would be a few tough days ahead. She was just grateful to have finally found her daughter.

Chapter Twenty-Two

"I suppose that is expected." Kerry's lips dropped as it was difficult to muster even a small smile.

"Don't take it personally. I think she never asked because she thought it would affect her mother and me if she admitted wanting to find her birth mother. Ella is what you would call an empath. She feels like she has a responsibility to spare others from experiencing pain and disappointment on her account. No matter how we told her it was okay if she had questions, she never tried to talk about it."

Kerry's heart sank. *How will I be able to get through to her if she hadn't even asked about me once?*

"You just have to take it one step at a time," Ethan encouraged as if reading her thoughts. "I'll set up a meeting between you and Ella. You just have to show up and explain what happened. Let fate take it from there."

"I guess you're right," she responded, a thin smile gracing her lips.

"I think you need time to process all that you've learned

and to prepare to talk to Ella. Why don't we set up the meeting for tomorrow?"

"I'd like that," she agreed.

Shortly after, Ethan left.

Kerry chose to take a shower and prepare to go to the bakery. She was sure Anne was wondering where she was as she was supposed to be at the bakery over an hour ago. She had contemplated not going in and remaining at home to wallow in self-pity, but she fought against that feeling. She needed to keep herself occupied.

A half hour later, she left the apartment, and in twenty minutes, she was pushing open the bakery's door.

"I'm sorry I'm late. I had an emergency," were the first words out of her mouth as she entered the kitchen. She quickly pulled on her apron and rushed to the sink to clean her hands.

"I was about to send out a search party when I didn't hear from you," Anne revealed.

"I should have called and let you know I was going to be late. I'm sorry about that. It slipped my mind."

Anne paused her kneading of the dough on the flat iron table to look over at Kerry, her observant eyes searching her face. Kerry gave her a quizzical look.

"As long as you're okay," the woman said, turning back to the dough.

Kerry rushed to the refrigerator to remove the items she needed for the chocolate mocha cake she was going to make. She spent the next half hour prepping and putting the ingredients together before running the batter into the spring tins she was using. She placed them into the already heated oven and set the timer.

She looked up at the clock to see that in five minutes, the bakery would be opened to the public.

"I'm gonna man the front this morning," she told Anne.

"Okay, honey," Anne replied.

"Oh, I forgot. I got some news today."

"What kind of news," Anne asked, raising her brows skeptically.

"The kind of news that means Heavenly Treats will remain in business for a very long time. Major Corp won't be building in Oak Harbor anymore. All small business owners this side are safe."

"That is wonderful news," the older woman smiled, pleased. "That gentleman of yours came through then."

"He's not my...we're not involved, Anne," she rushed out.

"I never said you were," the woman replied, giving her an innocent look. "I'm merely mentioning that he is a fine gentleman whom you have been spending a considerable amount of time with."

Kerry folded her lips in on each other, shaking her head. "You, Miss Anne, are a riot." She made her way out to the front to prepare for the arrival of customers. Three hours, that was how long Kerry had been on her feet. The morning crowd had somehow seemed to double, and she had not gotten more than a few minutes of reprieve. Her feet were aching, and she could literally feel her arms going slightly numb from working the cash register and serving the customers. She was happy when the rush of people seeking to curb their sweet tooth dwindled to know one coming through the door. Just as she was about to take a seat behind the display area, the chimes above the door jingled, bringing her attention to the person coming through it.

"Hi," the gentleman greeted, walking up to the counter.

"Hi, Darren," Kerry returned, waiting for him to speak further.

"I have an update on the matter at the office," he informed her.

"I'm guessing this is yet again information that could not be relayed by a phone call?" she asked, raising her brow.

Fall is in the Air

"I didn't want to because I'm not sure to what extent these people are monitoring our interactions," he explained.

"Okay then," Kerry responded simply, not truly buying his explanation. "I was just about to take a seat and have something to eat. Do you need anything?"

Darren looked down at the display case before looking back at her. "I'll have a serving of your apple strudel and a water," he ordered, removing a twenty-dollar bill from his pocket.

She rang up his order before taking out three pieces of the flaky, powdered pastries and placing them in a small pastry box.

"All right, Darren, what's the four-one-one?"

Her ex-husband took a bite of the strudel, nodding in approval as she chewed the strudel with its spicy apple filling. "This is great. It tastes different from other strudels I've had in a very good way."

Kerry stared wide-eyed at the man sitting across from her. No matter the occasion, Ethan had never complimented her. To think of it, he'd never had anything from the bakery since it had been in operation,

"Why did you come again?" she asked him to distract herself from thinking too much about his sudden interest in her goods.

"It's Irena. I think she might be innocent in all of this."

She drew back, surprised. "Are you sure?" she asked.

"Look," he said, removing sheets of paper from the brown envelope she hadn't registered he had on him.

Kerry took the sheets of paper with time stamps and dates on them. She skimmed the first page before looking up at him in question.

"It's all the employers who've had access to the building after business hours. It includes the security team and janitors. I circled Irena's name in blue and a few other names that are questionable."

Kerry looked back down at the file and skipped through the

pages noting the names circled. "What does this mean?" she asked.

"I took a look at the dates that Irena supposedly used her access pass to get into the building, and two of the days just do not make sense because she was in Hawaii visiting her parents for their golden anniversary. I know because I was the one who purchased the tickets for her."

Kerry pondered Darren's reasoning.

"But if she was in Hawaii, it means someone had access to her card, possibly someone very close to her if she hadn't reported it to be missing."

"That's the thing. When she came back from Hawaii, she mentioned that she couldn't find it, and we were going to deactivate it and give her a new one, but it showed up just like that. She just blamed it on her forgetfulness."

Kerry continued to nod as she contemplated.

"I then found out, by accident really, that she was dating someone from the IT department and that he'd visited her on two occasions at the office."

"You're right. If they were in collusion, she would have kept silent about their relationship. Maybe she really is innocent."

"Yes, so that means we're closer to solving this mystery than we were, or at least I hope so."

Kerry inclined her head in agreement.

"Have you heard from Emma?" he asked.

"Yes, I spoke with her yesterday. She said she was on her way to Austria."

"Okay, that's good. I haven't heard from her in two days, and she had promised to check in every twenty-four hours. That's the stipulation. That was what we had agreed on when I allowed her to go. This is the fourth time she's gone over the agreed time." Darren released an exasperated breath.

"You can't keep treating her like a child, Darren," Kerry spoke in frustration. "She agreed to check in, but things happen that may prove to derail her plans to check in with you on a set schedule like that. Just because you're the one paying for her trip doesn't mean you get to treat her like a child. She's more than that, and you'll lose her if you keep acting like her drill sergeant rather than her father." She was breathing hard at the end of her admonition.

Anger and resentment flashed in his hazel eyes. She could sense that he was biting back his retort. This was how she remembered their relationship. Him disagreeing with everything she said or did, holding her mistakes against her and monitoring everything that she did just so that he could have something to hold over her. It was the same thing he was doing to his youngest daughter, perhaps because Emma was so much more free-spirited like her. Kerry hated it.

"I think it's time for you to go, Darren." She stood, indicating that their conversation was over. Darren opened his mouth as if to respond but quickly shut it and stood.

"I'll let you know if I find anything else about the case," was all he said before walking out the door.

Kerry released a long, drawn-out breath and her shoulders sagged. She couldn't believe that she had remained married to him for so long. The only good thing that had resulted from their union, however, were their two daughters, who were the best versions of both of them.

The vibrating phone caught her attention, and she reached into her pocket to retrieve it. Her heart rate picked up pace when she saw the name of the caller.

"Hi," she greeted. "Okay, I'll see you tomorrow."

She hung up her call with Ethan feeling both anxious and hopeful.

* * *

Kerry held on to the steering wheel as a wave of anxiety steamrolled her. She felt on the verge of either passing out or throwing up. The engine remained idle, and she tried to calm her breathing to match the light and steady purring of the machine.

"All right, Kerry, you can do this. You can do this," she pep-talked herself as her head rested against the steering wheel. "You can do this." She raised her head to look in the rearview mirror. Reaching up, she wiped at the perspiration that had caused her short hair to stick against her forehead.

She jumped at the knock on her window. She turned to see Ethan there with concern etched on his face. She quickly rolled down her window.

"Hey," he greeted softly.

"Hey," she greeted back, her voice coming out small and timid.

"Are you sure you want to do this today?" he asked, scratching the back of his head and looking from her to the inn.

"No...I need to do this," she informed him. Cutting the car's engine, she stepped out.

Her knees felt as if they would buckle under the pressure of holding up her body.

"Kerry," Ethan spoke once more, his voice full of caution.

"I have to do this today," she resolved, looking up at him with pleading green eyes.

Ethan's gray eyes widened, and his Adam's apple bobbed in his throat as he gulped fresh air. "Okay, Ella's by the gazebo. I'll take you there," he said.

Kerry followed him through the inn's lobby. She waved hello to Marg, who was standing at the reception desk with Cora and the others she had hired more than a month ago to give Marg the opportunity to assume her role as manager. Ethan led her through the large mahogany door and down the paved path that led to the gazebo.

Fall is in the Air

Kerry's heart crashed against her chest as she looked at her daughter sitting among the pillows, her head down in a book.

She swallowed forcefully, wetting her dry trachea.

Ella, as if sensing them, raised her head and a bright smile graced her lips as she waved at Kerry, who was now finding it difficult to walk.

Chapter Twenty-Three

"Hi, Kerry. How are you?" Ella stood the moment Kerry walked under the gazebo

"Hi, Ella," she managed to respond, keeping the quiver from her voice as best as she could.

"I'll leave you ladies to talk."

"Okay, Dad."

Kerry looked back at Ethan with pleading eyes, willing him to stay. She needed the emotional support his presence offered.

"I have a few calls that I need to make," he gave as a way of excuse.

Kerry made to protest.

"I'll be close by," he promised.

She nodded in understanding, but the panic rooted her to the spot as she watched him walk back to the main house.

"Are you all right?"

Kerry turned to see her daughter staring back at her with concern in her green eyes.

"I'm fine," she lied, plastering a smile on her face as she walked over to where Ella stood. "Let's sit."

Fall is in the Air

Ella returned to the sectional and sank back among the cushions. Kerry sat across from her in one of the Adirondack chairs. She clasped and unclasped her hands before her as she tried to formulate her words. She had prepared her speech last night and recited it to herself until she fell asleep and even on her way over to the inn but now that Ella sat before her looking so innocent and unaware of how much her life was about to change because of her revelation, Kerry's throat clogged up with untethered fear.

"If you want, I can give you some time to collect your thoughts," Ella offered, giving her a sympathetic look.

"That's fine, I'm okay," Kerry assured her. After a few more seconds, she began. "I want to tell you a story."

"All right," Ella responded, her expression confused.

"It will all make sense, I promise."

Ella gestured for her to continue.

"There was this seventeen-year-old girl who was very happy and free-spirited. She met and fell in love with a rock star, and despite her parents being against the relationship, especially her father, the girl was convinced that this was the real thing, true love. So, when her rock star boyfriend chose to take his act on the road, she decided that her place was with him. Instead of finishing high school, she ran away with him. It was good for a while, but then, it wasn't, and they parted ways. The girl found out she was pregnant after that." Kerry paused to look at Ella, who was listening to the story keenly, although her expression gave away nothing about what she was thinking.

"She tried to make it work. For the next seven months, she scrubbed toilets, waited tables, and did anything she could get in between because she was ready to build a life for herself and her baby. She was so naïve. She thought everything would be okay." Kerry sighed and leaned forward with her elbows resting on her thighs. She bowed her head and closed her eyes, trying to muster the courage to continue. She straightened up and started again.

"Eventually, it became too hard to hold on to both jobs, and she had to give up one, which meant her already meager rations became even more rationed, and she was on the verge of being thrown out of the apartment she was renting. So, swallowing her pride, she called her father, and he came for her, but he hadn't known that she was pregnant."

Kerry looked over at Ella again with a sad smile on her lips, regret in her eyes. "I had to choose between being a single mother who would struggle with no help or give my baby up for adoption so she would have a better life."

Ella's eyes widened, and she straightened against the cushions trying to understand what Kerry was saying.

"Are you saying this story is about you?" the young woman asked carefully.

Kerry nodded in confirmation as tears flowed down her face.

Ella simply stared at her, her mouth set in a grim line as she dared Kerry to confirm that the unasked question was indeed true.

Kerry swallowed against the lump in her throat, the heaviness in her heart begging her to retreat.

"I held my baby only once in my arms after her birth, and at the end of the day, she was taken to the couple who had signed up to adopt her. I was told that they were a lovely family who would treat her well. That was the last time I saw my baby girl until...until..."

Kerry looked at Ella, the tears blurring her vision.

"What are you saying?" Ella asked, her tone even and void of emotions.

Kerry reached into the small purse she had brought and produced a small jewelry box. Opening it, she pulled out the one half of a heart-shaped locket on the single-strand gold necklace.

Ella's eyes widened in surprise as they zeroed in on the jewelry before they shuttered.

"Where did you get that?" she asked, her voice composed.

"It's mine," Kerry responded. "I bought it and another one that fits this perfectly." Kerry looked into Ella's eyes, which were very much her own, as she said, "I bought them for my daughter and had them inscribed with her name, Sara Jessica."

Ella jumped up so quickly that Kerry leaned back in surprise.

"So, you're telling me that you're my mother, is that it? That you abandoned me as a baby and never once tried to find me?" Ella asked in a deathly tone, her eyes narrowed as she stared back at Kerry.

"I know, sweetie, I—"

"Don't call me that," Ella said through clenched teeth. The look on Ella's face shredded her heart.

Kerry wrung her hands in her lap as her tears began to blur her vision once more.

Kerry watched as Ella closed her eyes, her body tensing with pent-up rage. She remained like that until her breaths that had been harsh evened out and her shoulders visibly relaxed as she released her fists.

She looked at Kerry, her eyes void of emotion, glistened with unshed tears.

"I don't know what you hoped to accomplish here, but I wish you hadn't told me any of it." With that, Ella turned and walked away.

She felt as if she couldn't breathe. Her heart was breaking into a million little pieces at how much she had hurt her. In that instance, she regretted telling her. She put her face in her hands as the tears racked her body.

"Hey."

Kerry looked up to see Ethan looking down at her tenderly.

"She hates me," was all she could manage as she put her hands back over her face and sobbed.

"She doesn't hate you," Ethan spoke soothingly. "She just has a lot to process, but I know my daughter. She will come around. You just have to give her time."

His daughter. Her heart broke even further. Ella was indeed Ethan's daughter. He was the one who had grown her into the wonderful young woman she was— him and his now deceased wife— not her.

"Thank you." She gave him a half smile through her tears.

"For what?" Ethan asked carefully.

"For growing her into the wonderful young woman that she is. I probably wouldn't have been able to do that. Even if she never speaks to me again, I'm happy to know that she had wonderful parents, that she'll still have you."

Ethan looked down at Kerry, a small smile gracing his lips. He held out his hand to her, and after a brief hesitation, she allowed him to pull her from her seat. "You are still a terrific mother, Kerry. Don't sell yourself short. You might not have gotten the chance to grow Ella, but you have two wonderful daughters who are proof that you are," he encouraged, holding her hands in his as he spoke.

Kerry smiled at him gratefully. "Thank you," she replied, her eyes wide with gratitude.

"No need to thank me. I am simply stating the truth."

After a minute of them standing there in silence, Kerry asked, "What do I do now?"

"You wait." Ethan gave each of her hands an encouraging squeeze. "When she's ready to talk, I'll let you know."

Kerry nodded. She left the inn feeling relieved and empty at the same time. She wasn't sure what she had expected, but Ella's reaction and her words had cut her deep.

Instead of turning onto the highway and heading home, she made a U-turn and made her way toward her parents' home.

When she made it, she paused with her arms on the steering wheel, the same as she had done at the inn earlier. When she was sure she had her emotions in check, she alighted from the car and made her way to the porch.

Maria answered the door after the second ring. "Hi, sweetie. I wasn't expecting you today," she greeted her daughter, reaching up to plant a kiss on her cheek.

"Hi, Mom. I wasn't planning on coming here either," she revealed.

Maria stared at her in confused surprise.

"Oh?"

"I'm actually here to talk to Dad— to both of you actually," she revealed.

"Well, your father is outside in the toolshed. I'll go call him."

Kerry nodded her approval.

She went into the family room to await her parents' arrival. As she paced back and forth, her eyes caught a picture over the mantle of the fireplace. Walking over, she took the frame in her hands. She ran a finger over the faces smiling back at her. It was a picture of her and her siblings and their children. They were all smiling happily at the camera. All the children were accounted for except one, her oldest daughter.

"Hi, sweetie. Are you all right? Your mother said you wanted to speak with us urgently?"

Kerry put the frame back in position before turning to the two people staring back at her with concern. She decided to cut straight to the chase.

"I found my daughter, and she's here in Oak Harbor."

The audible gasps and the synchronized looks of surprise on her parents' faces would have merited a chuckle from her if the matter wasn't so serious.

Luke was the first to recover from the initial shock. "What do you mean she's in Oak Harbor? Is she looking for you?"

"No, she isn't. It turns out that we already met without either of us knowing that we were related. Up until yesterday, we would have crossed paths many more times with none being the wiser."

"Who is it?" Luke asked, his brows furrowed.

"Her name is Ella Sharpe, the girl whose father was working with Major Corp. They were at the barbecue."

At her revelation, the room plunged into shocked silence. If a pin had been dropped at that moment, it would have echoed throughout the halls.

"Are you sure?" Luke finally asked.

"I am," she responded. "The PI gave me all the information I needed, and Ethan confirmed that he and his wife adopted her through the adoption agency in Houston."

Luke sat on the couch and rested a hand against his cheek. Maria sat beside him.

"You didn't tell her, did you?"

Kerry looked at her father in incredulity. "Are you serious right now?"

"Kerry-Ann," her father spat in a warning tone.

She visibly relaxed. As irritated as she was by him, she still respected him and her mother, and this was their home.

"I asked because I want you to be sure this is what you want to do— what you think is best."

"Like you gave me a choice twenty-three years ago?" She gave him a deadpan look. It was taking everything in her not to shout.

"What is that supposed to mean?"

"It means that if you had supported me and told me that it would have been okay if I chose to keep my baby, then we wouldn't be in this situation today," she said tightly.

"I was looking out for your future, Kerry-Ann. I saw how

down you were, how tired and out of touch you were with... everything. It was like this pregnancy was a death sentence, and I didn't want you to end up resenting your child for holding you back from accomplishing what you wanted to achieve. I did it for both of you."

"It wasn't your decision to make, Dad!" she blew up. "You guilted me into making the worse decision of my life all because I didn't want to be a screwup in your eyes, and now I don't know if Ella will ever want to speak to me. What I regret most was ever listening to you."

She turned her back and walked away from her parents and out of the house. She needed to be alone and process the events of the day.

Chapter Twenty-Four

Kerry reached over to her bedside table to get her vibrating phone.
"Hello?"
"Hi, sweetie."
She sat up in bed, resting her back against the upholstered headboard. "Hi, Mom."
"Is this a good time to talk? It sounds like you're still in bed."
"I can talk," she assured her mother.
"Okay."
After a few seconds of silence and Kerry wondering if her mother was going to say what she wanted to hear, Maria spoke.
"I'm sorry that I never got more involved in the decision you had to make, Kare Bear...I am a mother, and I know how hard that decision must have been for you. I failed you as your mother."
"Mom," Kerry started.
"No. Please...let me finish," Maria pleaded. Kerry remained silent. "I wanted to come to you when you were in Houston,

Fall is in the Air

but you were adamant that I didn't need to come, that you just needed your father...you were always a daddy's girl. I convinced myself that when you were ready, when the time was right, you would ask for me, but you never did. Then I found out that you were pregnant and that the decision had already been made to give the baby up for adoption, and the papers had been signed." Maria sighed. "I was so angry with your father. For a long time, I couldn't even look at him for what he did, but he tried, and he worked hard to be better. That's why he doted on his grandchildren, trying to make up for what happened. Only it didn't work when you came back. You started making all the choices he would have been proud of, even marrying Darren. I could see that you weren't happy, but you became so closed off. You never shared anything with me, and I didn't know how to reach you."

There was another pause followed by a few sniffles. Kerry's heart constricted.

"What I am trying to say, sweetie, is that I'm sorry I didn't fight harder to be there for you. I want you to know that whatever decision you make, I will always support it because you deserve to be happy."

"Thanks, Mom." Kerry breathed out, holding her hand to her heart. "I appreciate that, and I love you very much."

"I love you too, sweetie. So much."

"I know," Kerry responded.

After the two finished talking, Kerry went to take a shower and prepare for the day. Today she would be telling her daughters about their older sister. Her nerves increased tenfold at the knock sounding at the door.

That meant Sophia had arrived. She had been staying with her father the past couple of days but had agreed to come over to talk with her.

"Hi, Mom," Sophia greeted, accepting her mother's hug.

"Hi, sweetie. Where's your key?"

"I forgot it. I had a lot on my mind," Sophia responded, entering the apartment.

"Did you tell your sister that I wanted to talk to her?"

"I did. She's on standby."

"Good," Kerry said, even as her heart continued to beat rapidly against her chest.

"Mom, are you okay?"

Kerry looked over at her daughter, staring back at her in concern.

"I am, sweetie. I just have some difficult news to tell you and your sister, and I don't know how you'll take it," she spoke honestly.

"Mom, you're scaring me," Sophia said worriedly. "You're not sick, are you?"

"No, honey. I'm fine. What I have to tell you is something I've never spoken about to anyone except my parents."

Sophia inclined her head in understanding but still stared at her mother skeptically. The phone rang, and Sophia answered it.

"Hey, Sis. Yeah, she's here and ready. I'll put you on speaker."

Sophia put the phone on speaker before putting it on the coffee table.

"Hi, Mom," Emma greeted.

"Hi, sweetie. How are you?"

"I'm good. Better since yesterday, actually. Did you say something to Dad? He's been extra nice about me missing our check-in time."

"Maybe your father finally realizes that you're not a little girl anymore, honey," Kerry responded, evading the original question.

"Maybe," Emma replied, her voice still unsure. "Anyway, what's the big news that you have to tell us?" She gasped. "You didn't get married, did you?"

Fall is in the Air

"Of course not." Kerry laughed at her daughter's antics. She sobered up shortly afterward. "I'm happy that I'm able to share this information with you both even though I wish you were here in person, Emma."

Her daughters remained silent, waiting for her to continue.

"I got pregnant at seventeen and gave birth to a daughter at eighteen," she told them, ripping the Band-Aid right off.

She saw Sophia furrow her brows as if she was working out a difficult math problem.

"I'm twenty," she said thoughtfully. "If you had me when you were eighteen, then that would make me twenty-three." Sophia's eyes widened in surprise, and Kerry nodded to answer her question.

"I have another child, a daughter who's twenty-three."

"Where?"

"How?"

Kerry attempted to answer her daughters' questions.

"In Houston, Texas. I ran away with my boyfriend of the time, but we broke up, and I found out I was pregnant." She paused, looking at Sophia apologetically. "I gave her up for adoption, but fate brought her back into my life."

"You found her?" Sophia asked, surprised.

Kerry nodded. "Turns out Ella is my daughter," she broke the news.

Sophia stared wide-eyed, her lips parted and immobile.

"Who is Ella?" Emma asked from over the receiver.

Sophia shook her head, recovering her composure.

"Did you know?" she asked.

Kerry shook her head.

"I only found out two days ago."

"Guys, who is Ella?"

"Ella is my biological daughter, sweetie. She's on a term break and visiting with her father."

"Mom took them sightseeing, and they came to the

barbecue last week," Sophia added.

"Wow, this is crazy," Ella replied, shocked. "I have a sister that's older than you, Sophia. How cool is that?"

Sophia rolled her eyes.

"Are you all right, sweetie?" Kerry asked cautiously.

"Yes, I'm okay." Sophia smiled. "It's a lot to take in, but I am also thrilled. Ella is a nice person. I hope we can get to know each other better."

"I hope so, too, honey," Kerry agreed, a slight panic rising within her as she wasn't sure if Ella would want to meet or interact with them.

She was surprised at how well her children had taken the news. Neither of them had resented her but had chosen to understand what she'd been through. After an hour of talking and joking, Sophia left to go to her father.

Kerry sat on the couch, going through the album that captured the moments of her life, from birth to her wedding to having her children and recording their achievements. The only era of her life that was not in print was her time with Mark, her time struggling to provide for her and her baby, and the day she had to let her go. Tears slipped down her cheeks as her mind went back to how hurt Ella had looked, how her eyes had accused her of abandoning her. She clutched the album to her chest, wishing she could fill it with memories of her oldest daughter.

The knock at the front door brought her out of her pitiful wallowing. Placing the album on the coffee table, she pulled her cardigan around her and used the sleeve to wipe at the moisture on her face.

She opened the door to see Tessa, Cora, Andrea, and Josephine at her door. She furrowed her brows. "What are you guys doing here?" she asked.

"We heard what happened," Tessa replied, her face marred with sadness as she stared at her sister.

Kerry couldn't help herself. She broke down in tears, and Tessa reached for her, hugging her tightly against her as tears rolled down her own cheeks.

"I wish I had known, Sis. I can't believe you had to go through all of this by yourself," Tessa cried. "You have been through so much, and I didn't even know."

"It's okay," Kerry assured her. "I'm just happy that you're here now."

After the two separated, her cousins reached out and hugged her as well.

"Unless we're planning to camp out in the hallway, I suggested we head inside," Andrea said, not so subtly looking over her shoulder at Kerry's neighbor, Mrs. Dorsey. The woman was always at her door, posted like security, watching everything that happened.

Her sister and cousins filed into the room and closed the door, locking out her nosy neighbor. They made their way into the kitchen, opening a bottle of Cabernet.

"I can't believe that young lady is your daughter. It's just surreal," Andrea said, taking a sip of the red wine they brought for the occasion along with a whole tub of Ben & Jerry's.

"Yeah. I remember we were saying how uncanny the resemblance was. She reminded us so much of you when you were that age," Cora told her.

"I'm still trying to process it," Kerry admitted. "I just wish I knew what to say to make her understand that I made a mistake, that I never really wanted to give her up." She sighed and ran her palm down the side of her face in frustration. Her sister rubbed her hand up and down her arm comfortingly. She looked over at her.

"You were still very young, Kerry. Practically a child. You did what you thought you had to do, what you thought was best for her. No one should hold that against you. Just give her time," she encouraged.

"That's what Ethan said." She sighed dejectedly.

The sisters exchanged looks before Cora suggested, "Why don't we have a pajama party? It'll be like when we were kids."

Kerry thought about it.

"You need something to distract you even for a little while," Josephine said, giving her an encouraging smile.

"All right," she agreed. "But where are you going to get pajamas? I've only got two good pairs. The others are filled with holes and cut-outs."

"Not a problem," Tessa chimed in. "We'll wear whatever you have. That's why we're called a family, remember?"

Kerry grinned appreciatively at the women, happy to have such a great circle of family members that were also her closest friends. "Thanks, guys," she said, receiving all the hugs they gave.

After freshening up and donning the pajamas Kerry gave them, they moved the coffee table to the side and filled the carpeted floor with throw pillows and cushions as they watched reruns of *I Love Lucy*. They laughed and joked as if there were no tomorrow. The wine they were sipping provided them with the right amount of buzz, and the chocolate ice cream boosted their serotonin.

"So, I heard that Major Corp is looking outside of Oak Harbor for their ventures, and Ethan is to be thanked for that," Cora mentioned.

"Yeah, he told me."

Kerry looked over at her cousin and noticed that all eyes were actually turned on her.

"What?" she asked, feeling self-conscious.

"What's going on between you two?" Andrea asked directly.

"Nothing. We're just friends, and as it turns out, we both share the same daughter," she defended.

"And there aren't any feelings there?"

This time it was Tessa who asked.

"It's complicated." She sighed. "I don't think it's a good idea to get involved in any way, considering how much of a mess I've made everything."

"Kerry. You like him, and I can tell that he likes you very much. Despite the challenges, you deserve happiness, and you deserve to know if he can give you that. Don't run away and hide. Choose yourself. Choose your happiness."

Her heart warmed over at the earnestness in her sister's gaze.

"I'll try," she promised.

Her phone rang just then. She widened her eyes in surprise when she realized that Ethan was calling. "It's Ethan," she informed the curious eyes on her.

"Answer it," Andrea urged.

"Hi, Ethan." She cringed at how breathy and eager her voice sounded.

"Hi," he returned. "I didn't hear from you since yesterday. I was wondering if you're okay."

"I am," she replied. "Is there any update on Ella?"

Ethan hesitated. "No, she's still adamant that she doesn't want to talk about it."

"Oh."

"She'll come around. Give her time."

"Time," they both said at the same time.

After a short pause, he began to speak again. "I actually wanted to go back to our conversation from the other day before all of this."

"I don't remember. Could you jog my memory?" she asked.

Another pause ensued before he said, "About us...I was serious about getting to know you better, Kerry."

Her heart fluttered, and her hand tightened around the phone.

"Have dinner with me."

Chapter Twenty-Five

"I can't believe I allowed you guys to talk me into going on this date," Kerry simpered as Andrea applied her makeup while Cora and Tessa rummaged through her closet.

"You agreed that you would give it a try, Kerry. Don't get cold feet now." Tessa came through the sliding door holding up a red, sweetheart neckline, off-the-shoulder dress with a fitted bodice that flared from the waist and an emerald, green form-fitting silk dress with spaghetti straps and draped at the front.

"The green dress," Andrea and Josephine agreed without hesitation.

After her sister and cousins had finished dolling her up, she stood before her floor-to-ceiling closet mirror, lips agape as she stared at her reflection.

"There is no way he'll be able to focus on dinner tonight with you looking so scrumptious," Andrea said from over her shoulder, giving her a once-over of approval.

"You're beautiful, Sis," Tessa affirmed.

Fall is in the Air

Kerry looked back at her sister and smiled gratefully. "Thanks."

There was a knock at the door.

"I'll get it," Cora offered, walking out of the bedroom.

"Are you ready?" Tessa asked encouragingly.

She nodded, not trusting her voice.

The women followed her out to the living room where Ethan stood talking to Cora, but the minute his gaze landed on Kerry, it remained glued on her, and she found that she couldn't look away from his magnetizing gray eyes.

"You look beautiful," were the first words out of his mouth the minute she was standing before him.

She could feel her cheeks flushing and was sure they were by now tinted red. "You look beautiful too... I mean, handsome."

She could hear the slight snicker behind her and wished that her family would just disappear into thin air.

"These are for you," he said, bringing her attention to the bouquet of yellow tulips he was holding.

"Thank you, these are lovely," she said, breathing in the faint flowery scent.

"We'll put them in water for you. I'm sure you both should be on your way now," Tessa spoke, taking the flowers from her hand and subtly pushing her toward Ethan.

"Are you ready to go?" he asked.

"Yes, I am." With that, she allowed Ethan to lead her outside the apartment and downstairs, all the while under the inquisitive eyes of her sister and cousins.

"Are you warm enough?" he asked her as he fiddled with the air conditioning controls.

"I am, thank you," she informed him.

Soon he was off. After more than five minutes, Ethan spoke, "Your sister and cousins are nice."

"They are," she agreed.

"You still haven't told me where we're going," she pointed out.

"That's because it is a surprise," Ethan looked at her with a smirk.

"Well, I love surprises, so it had better be worth it," she joked.

"Oh, trust me, it will be."

A half hour later, they were parked outside the marina. Ethan rounded the car door and held out his hand to her. Kerry took it, ignoring the warmth that ran from her fingertips all the way up her arm, and allowed him to guide her down the boardwalk, the path lit by lanterns.

Kerry turned to look at him questioningly, then back at the dock and then back at him. Ethan smiled charmingly down at her.

"Your chariot awaits, madam, or in this instance, your yacht."

"This is...wow," she expressed, at a loss for words.

"I see that it is shaping up to be a good surprise."

"It is," she replied, touching his arm affectionately. "If I forget to tell you later, I want you to know I had a great time."

Ethan smiled. "I am having a great time just being here with you."

Her smile blossomed as she blushed at his compliment.

Ethan helped her up the ramp as they boarded the boat.

"Welcome to the *Pacific*, my name is Manuel, and I will be your server this evening. The captain, Mr. Gomez, is at the helm, and he will be taking the yacht out into the bay so that you can enjoy your meal in the ambiance that open water creates."

Kerry shook the man's hand and allowed him to escort her and Ethan toward the front, where a table was already set for dinner under the amber glow of candles.

Fall is in the Air

Manuel seated them before excusing himself to get their food and wine.

"When did you do all of this?" Kerry asked, already bowled over by how great the date was going.

"Um, the day before we went on our hike over by Windjammer Park," he told her, scratching the back of his neck nervously.

"So, you were confident that I would have said yes then," she asked.

"No, not confident, but I was willing to bet that you would."

Kerry smiled. "I can't say I'm disappointed that you did this," she said, putting him at ease.

A broad smile graced his own lips.

Just then, Manuel appeared.

"This evening, we'll start out with the lemon butter scallops paired with a bottle of your choice of red wine for the evening." After setting the dishes before them, Manuel took out a bottle of Cabernet Sauvignon from the cooler.

Ethan and Kerry cheered when he popped the cork, and the mouth of the bottle smoked from the pressure release.

After pouring them each a glass, he excused himself once more.

"Let's play a game," Kerry suggested, grinning over the table at her date.

"What do you have in mind?" he asked.

Her eyes twinkled. "Let's play two truths and one lie."

"All right, shoot."

Kerry placed her recently manicured fingernail against the corner of her lips as she thought about her answers. "Okay, let's go. I was the captain of the cheerleading squad in high school, I broke my arm in the third grade, and I went swimming with the sharks in Hawaii."

Ethan's brows furrowed as he considered her responses. "I

can definitely see you being a cheerleader in high school, and you very well could have broken your hand in elementary school, but swimming with sharks, eh? I'm not sure you would do something like that even though I know that you love adventures. Still, I don't see you in such a high-stress situation."

"What is your final answer?" Kerry asked, smirking at him.

"I'm gonna say the shark-infested waters is not true."

Kerry chortled. "I somehow knew that you wouldn't believe that answer to be true."

"Is it true?" he asked, his eyes widening in surprise.

"It is," she affirmed with a smirk.

"So, which one is fake," he asked, a perplexed expression on his face.

"I was never a cheerleader."

"What?" he asked disbelievingly.

"I was more into sports than cheers in high school."

"You really surprise me."

"All right, your turn."

Ethan took some time to think about his answers before staring mischievously at her. "I have a black belt in karate. I was super nerdy in high school and..." He stared seriously at her, his unwavering stare causing her face to heat up.

"What?" she asked, her voice barely audible.

"I was smitten by you from the first time I saw you."

Kerry inhaled sharply as her chest filled with considerable warmth from the excessive thumping of her heart.

"Is that one of your answers?" she managed to ask.

"Yes... it is," he spoke confidently.

"I'm guessing I can't choose that as my answer then." She breathed out.

Ethan's lips curled into a smile as his eyes remained focused on her.

"I don't think you were a nerdy high schooler, but I do believe you have your black belt."

"What is your answer then?" he asked, leaning forward.

"I am going to say you weren't a nerdy kid ever."

It was Ethan's time to chuckle. "I wore glasses and had braces all the way up to tenth grade, and I played the accordion in the band."

"I don't believe you," Kerry snorted.

"It's true." Ethan laughed.

"I would have loved to see that," she told him.

"Trust me, you can. I have a whole album dedicated to my awkward years," he promised.

"I'll hold you to that."

For the next hour, they enjoyed the delicious meal and light conversation. After they ate, Ethan led her toward the foredeck. They stood looking out at the dark waters that shimmered brightly in the path of the moon.

"Did you mean what you said about me?"

Ethan turned one hundred and eighty degrees to look down at her. Kerry turned to look back at him.

"What did I say?"

She couldn't see his eyes, but she could imagine the intensity of their gaze on her.

"You said you were smitten with me from the first time you saw me. Did you mean it?"

Ethan reached down to run the tip of his index across her temple, which caused her to shiver. "I wouldn't have said it if I didn't mean it," he spoke simply. "The first time I saw you stand up and speak your mind at the town hall meeting, I was enthralled by how passionate you were defending your business and the rights of your fellow business owners. You were unapologetic but authentic, and I felt drawn to you. Although it was a coincidence that I happened to enter your bakery and speak with you, I wanted to know more about you. I wanted to be in your presence for however long you would have me. I am utterly smitten by you, Kerry." Ethan reached down to raise her hand to his chest. "I know you might not be there, that it might be too soon, but I am falling in love with you."

Kerry stared up at the man baring his soul to her. She felt rooted at this moment with him, and her heart felt as if it would burst from the emotions seated in her chest.

"Ethan...I don't know what to say other than I know it's too soon, and there is so much that we're dealing with because of the situation with Ella."

Ethan's shoulders fell as he prepared for her letdown.

"But I can't deny the fact that I have feelings for you too. I am falling in love with you too."

His smile glowed brightly under the low deck lights. His head dipped until their foreheads met. Kerry held her breath as he inched closer, their noses brushing and breaths mingled. Finally, their lips met, and it was as if a fire had been lit in her belly. Ethan cupped her face in his palm, bringing their lips closer until it felt as if they were breathing the same air. When they separated, Kerry gulped in the fresh air as she tried to calm her frenzied heart and overheated skin.

"Wow...that was..."

"Amazing," Ethan finished for her, smiling wide.

"Amazing," she agreed. She couldn't help the broad smile that split her own face. She felt deliriously happy at that moment— happy that she had met Ethan, happy that he brought her daughter back to her, and happy that she had agreed to the date.

"Excuse me. Are you ready for dessert?"

Kerry and Ethan separated to look at their server, who looked back at them expectantly. She felt as if she'd already had her dessert standing there with Ethan, but she was curious as to what had been prepared for them.

"It is a chocolate fondue and fruit," Manuel said as if he had read her mind.

Ethan led her back to the table, and they spent the rest of

Fall is in the Air

the evening enjoying the sweet chocolate-dipped fruits. They continued to have light banter as they brought the evening to a close.

When Ethan parked in her complex and let her out, she allowed him to hold her hand and walk her toward the lobby. The doorman stopped her before she entered.

"Excuse me, Miss Hamilton. There's a young lady here to see you. She's been waiting for the past hour."

She furrowed her brows, wondering who it could be.

"Thank you," she replied, walking into the lobby.

The second her gaze landed on who was waiting on her, her eyes became saucers.

Her daughter stared back at her before her eyes averted to the hand-holding ones. Kerry quickly pulled her hand out of Ethan's as if she'd been caught stealing.

"Did you know she was coming here?" she turned and whispered.

"No, she didn't say, but I did tell her that I asked you out on a date. I don't keep anything from her," he informed her. "I feel like this is where our date will end. You both have a lot to talk about."

Kerry nodded, grateful for the time to compose herself.

"I'll call you later," Ethan promised, placing a soft kiss against her cheek.

She walked toward the young woman staring unblinkingly at her, then stopped before her.

"Hi, Ella."

Chapter Twenty-Six

Kerry stood against the wall, her stomach in knots as she watched her daughter walk around her living room. She stopped by the display mantle, laden with photos of her and her two other daughters and the rest of the family. She held her breath, waiting for whatever accusation was coming her way.

"You have a very lovely family," Ella turned to say.

Kerry's mouth opened in surprise at her observation.

"They're very loyal. I remember thinking that when I met them last week at the barbecue, they were so happy to be around each other, and I felt happy to be around them. I hadn't felt that way in a long time. Not since my mom died."

Kerry's heart broke at the pain reflected in her tone when talking about her adoptive mother. "Would you like to talk about her?" she offered.

Ella stiffened, and Kerry wished she hadn't said anything.

"My mom was a happy person," Ella said, surprising her.

Kerry gestured for her to take a seat, and she took a seat across from her and waited for her to continue.

"She used to tell me that I was her miracle from God and that I was destined for great things. She helped me with every project, listened to every argument I had, and allowed my questions. When I started playing mini-league softball, she was at every one of my games. She promised that no matter what, she would always be my number one fan, cheering me on because I was destined for greatness." Ella released a shaky breath as she stared down at her clasped hands.

Kerry itched to go over and hug her to her chest, to tell her that she was there for her. Instead, she sat quietly, waiting for her to continue.

"When she got sick, she and dad tried to shield me from it, but I could tell that something was wrong, especially when she became too tired to leave the bed and when she started eating away from the table. When they finally sat me down and explained what was happening, that she might not get better, I just shut off. I couldn't function at school. I became closed off from everyone, so Dad chose to homeschool me for the duration of her illness so that I could remain close to her. I was right there on the bed with her when she took her last breath. I cried because my mother was gone, and she wouldn't see me grow up and achieve my dreams. She wouldn't see me get married or get to spoil her grandchildren."

"I'm so sorry that you had to go through that, Ella. I can't imagine how devastated you were and to have lost her at such a young age," she soothed.

Ella looked up at her, her expression pained.

"When I found out that you were my biological mother, I was angry."

Kerry reared back, her words stabbing at her.

"I was angry at you for giving me up and then just coming back into my life like that. But...I was more upset with myself," she finished, bowing her head in guilt. "I was angry at myself for the relief I felt when you told me that you were my mother," she spoke softly.

This time Kerry reached across the small space to rest her hand over Ella's. The girl turned her green eyes to Kerry, which were a mirror of her own.

"I felt like I was betraying her memory by wanting to get to know you. I almost didn't come. I was on the verge of packing my bags and returning to my dorm, but then Mr. Hamilton, my grandfather, showed up and explained that you weren't at fault. He said that he made it impossible for you to choose to keep me and how much it has affected you all this time. He said if I wanted to blame anyone, it should be him."

Kerry was surprised that her father would have taken such a step to try to mend her relationship with her daughter, and she was touched that he went as far as confessing his role in her being given up for adoption.

"I really want you to know that if I could go back to that day, I never would have given you up. I would have chosen to keep you.

"It's okay," Ella assured her. "I don't know how my life would have turned out if I wasn't adopted by my parents, but being here now and experiencing the love that I had with them, I don't think I would ever change that," she answered truthfully.

Kerry reached up to run her hand down her daughter's cheek in a loving manner. "I'm glad that you got the parents you deserved too."

Ella smiled.

"I know it might be a big ask, but I would like us to get to know each other, and I would like my family to be formally introduced to you as long as you're fine with it."

"I am," she agreed, which brought a smile to her face. "There's one more thing that I would like to know.

"Okay," Kerry invited.

Fall is in the Air

"What can you tell me about my father?"

She couldn't say she was surprised by the question, but it still floored her.

"Um, well, his name was Mark Sinclair, and he was the lead singer of a rock and roll band. He was pretty good and was on the verge of superstardom, but he partied hard. He passed away a long time ago from an overdose. I'm sorry it couldn't have been better news. If you want, I can try and help you to find his family."

"That's all right," Ella assured her. "I'm already starting off a new relationship with you. I think it's better to take it one step at a time."

Kerry nodded her agreement. The two spent another hour talking, Kerry mostly answering her questions. When she left, it was way past midnight, but Ella promised to call her when she got back to the inn.

The next morning, Kerry woke feeling refreshed. If this was what it felt like when people said that they had a new lease on life, then she wasn't complaining. She was overcome with joy knowing that her daughter was willing to try to have a relationship with her. Her mind flashed to what Ella had said about her father visiting her. She realized that she had him to thank for Ella choosing to give her a call.

After taking a shower, Kerry put on a pair of blue jeans and tucked a white shirt into the waist before pushing her feet into a pair of flats. She decided to stop by her parents' home before heading to the bakery. She needed to get everything together for the Halloween party later, but she really needed to talk to her dad first.

"Hi, honey," her mother greeted, surprised once more to see her daughter at the front door after the blowout that had happened less than a week ago.

"Hi, Mom," Kerry said with a broad smile before placing a kiss on her cheek.

Maria stared at her daughter, confused. "Is everything okay?" she asked carefully.

"Everything's fine, Mom." She grinned. "I just wanted to talk to Dad. Is he here?"

"He's in the kitchen," Maria informed her, her gaze darting inside the house before looking back at her daughter with a worried expression.

"Don't worry, Mom, I'm only here to thank him for what he did with Ella," she assured the woman.

"Oh, okay," Maria replied, her voice reflecting her uncertainty.

Maria followed her into the kitchen, where Luke was under the kitchen sink. "Hi, Dad. Have you made any progress under there?" she called out.

Luke pulled his head from under the sink to look at his daughter.

"I see you're still tinkering with things that you have no business tinkering with," she joked.

"I'll have you know that I have a certificate in plumbing," her father revealed, coming to his feet. "How are you?" he asked after some time of them just staring at each other.

"I'm fine," she said, giving him a small smile. "I wanted to thank you for what you did with Ella...for talking to her, I mean." She sat on the bar stool around the island.

Luke walked over to stand before her, his eyes full of remorse. "I've had some time to think about how my actions have affected you for so long, and I want to say I am sorry from the bottom of my heart." Luke brought his hand to his chest as he gave his heartfelt speech. "I don't know how I could have made you do that. You're my daughter, and I promised to protect you, but I broke that trust and perpetuated your hurt for so long. I now know that I was wrong to do that, Kare Bear. I hope you can find it in your heart to forgive me."

"I already have, Dad." She smiled. "I know you thought you

were doing the right thing back then, but I'm glad that you were able to step into my shoes and understand me."

At this, Luke rounded the island and pulled his daughter into a tight hug. "I love you so much, Kerry. I'll spend the rest of my life making up for the hurt I caused you and my granddaughter."

"I love you too, Daddy." Kerry grinned against his chest, her heart swelling with happiness.

* * *

Kerry fixed the fairy wings of her Tinker Bell costume for the third time that evening.

"Are you sure you don't want to go put on the other costume?"

Kerry looked over at Ethan in his Peter Pan costume, staring down at her with concern.

"I'm fine," she promised, grinning for added reassurance. "I just might take off the wings and be a wingless fairy, though," she informed him.

"You'll still be the prettiest fairy I've ever seen," he whispered against her ear. She shivered as a smile appeared on her lips. Putting her arms around his shoulder, she stared into his eyes. "You can say that again. I don't mind," she invited.

Ethan dipped his head to peck her lips. "You are the fairest of them all," he reiterated, pecking her lips once more.

"Is this what you two call dancing or are you too far gone to even try and sway to the music?"

Kerry laughed as she looked over at Andrea in a Wilma Flintstone costume and her boyfriend Donny, dressed as Fred Flintstone. Unlike them, the couple was moving to the beat of the music as a disco ball cast colorful shadows on the floor. Cora and Jo were also on the dance floor with their men, and like Andrea, they kept in beat with the music.

"Do you want to sit?" Ethan asked.

"Yes," she agreed, allowing him to lead her through the dancing bodies to their table at the back. Tessa sat by the table dressed as Cruella de Vil and looking bored.

"Remind me why did I allow you to drag me from my perfectly comfortable bed to come to a party that I can't enjoy again," she said the moment they slid into the booth.

"I told you to come out on the dance floor with us," Kerry pointed out.

Tessa smirked at her sister. "I'm not third wheeling. That's embarrassing, especially at my age."

"I'll go get us some punch," Ethan offered, giving them time to talk.

After some time, Tessa spoke.

"I've never seen you like this. You look very happy, Sis."

Kerry smiled. "I am."

Epilogue

Two weeks later

"I'd like to present a toast." Everyone stared at Luke, wondering why he had called their attention to him and the raised glass in his hands.

"Uncle Luke, you do know we're at a barbecue and not a dinner, right?"

Luke gave his grandnephew a dark glare before flashing a dazzling smile at the people before him.

"I know it isn't a formal dinner or anything like that, as Josh so graciously pointed out, and it's not Thanksgiving yet, but I want to express how thankful I am to see you all." He looked out at his family, a smile of appreciation gracing his lips. "Over six months ago, we were plagued by the sadness of losing Sam, but today as we stand here, I'm thankful that we were able to find our way home. I am thankful for the new addition like my own granddaughter, Ella." He raised his glass in Ella's direction.

"Family is everything. Something I have come to cherish

with all of my heart. So, as I stand here, I raise a glass to you all. Thank you for being a part of this family. Thank you for supporting this family. The Hamiltons will always thrive because we have each other."

At the end of his speech, those who had glasses or cans raised them in agreement.

Kerry smiled encouragingly when her father's gaze landed on her, and she mouthed, "great speech."

"Mom, did you know that Ella wants to be a neurosurgeon? That means she has another five years after this."

Kerry grinned at her youngest daughter, who appeared to be freaking out that her oldest sister had been in school for so many years.

"That's because she's dedicated," Kerry replied.

"I really like her mom. She's really nice."

At her daughter's revelation, a broad smile graced her lips. She was really happy to see her three girls getting along, especially knowing that Emma had returned from her travels just to meet Ella. Never in a million years could she have imagined that her life could have changed so drastically in such a short time, but it had, and it continued to get better. Her daughter was back in her life, and she already had a wonderful connection with her two sisters.

Even her relationship with Darren had improved, especially seeing that last week she helped him set up the trap that ensnared the gentleman who had been robbing the company blind. It had been a relief when they managed to clear his secretary's name also as she had just been a victim of circumstances, her so-called boyfriend using her to gain access to Darren's office.

"Penny for your thoughts?"

She turned her head to look at the gentleman standing at her side with a bright smile. Her lips split into a big grin. "I was just thinking of how happy I am."

"What are you happy about?" he asked, continuing to smile down at her.

She turned fully in his arms. "I'm happy for the first time in a long time. I have everything that I could ever want."

"And what is everything you could ever want?" he probed.

She turned and put her hands around his neck as she stared up at him. "I have a family that I love dearly. My daughter is back in my life and...I can't complain about the present company."

Ethan tipped his head and pecked her lips. "You're not so bad yourself," he quipped, pecking her one more time.

Kerry smiled and turned in his hand so that her back was to his chest. Again, she took in the scene before her."

"Did I tell you that I am thinking about opening an office here?"

She inclined her head to look up at him, surprised.

"You're really thinking about it?" she asked, grinning widely.

"I am," he returned. "I want to practice environmental law. I think this is the best place as any to do that...and I'm looking forward to having many adventures with you."

For the entire barbecue, her lips remained in a smiling position. Everything was finally in order, and she was ecstatic. Life couldn't get any better.

Coming Next in the Oak Harbor Series

You can pre order: A Spectacular Event

Other Books by Kimberly

The Archer Inn Series
An Oak Harbor Series
A Yuletide Creek Series

Connect with Kimberly Thomas

Facebook
Newsletter
BookBub

To receive exclusive updates from Kimberly, please sign up to be on her Newsletter!

Made in the USA
Monee, IL
05 March 2023